Gingersnap

ALSO BY PATRICIA REILLY GIFF

All the Way Home
Eleven
The Gift of the Pirate Queen
A House of Tailors
Lily's Crossing
Maggie's Door
Nory Ryan's Song
Pictures of Hollis Woods
R My Name Is Rachel
Storyteller
Water Street
Wild Girl
Willow Run

Gingersnap

Patricia Reilly Giff

WENDY
LAMB
BOOKS

Text copyright © 2013 by Patricia Reilly Giff
Jacket art copyright © 2013 by Kamil Vojnar

All rights reserved. Published in the United States by Wendy Lamb Books, an imprint of Random House Children's Books, a division of Random House, Inc., New York.

Wendy Lamb Books and the colophon are trademarks of Random House, Inc.

Visit us on the Web! randomhouse.com/kids

Educators and librarians, for a variety of teaching tools, visit us at RHTeachersLibrarians.com

Library of Congress Cataloging-in-Publication Data
Giff, Patricia Reilly.
Gingersnap / Patricia Reilly Giff.
p. cm.
Summary: When her brother Rob, a Navy cook, goes missing in action during World War II, Jayna, desperate for family, leaves upstate New York and their cranky landlandy, accompanied by a turtle and a ghost, to seek their grandmother, who Rob believes may live in Brooklyn. Includes soup recipes.
ISBN 978-0-375-83891-0 (hardback)—ISBN 978-0-375-93891-7 (lib. bdg)—ISBN 978-0-307-98029-8 (ebook) [1. Brothers and sisters—Fiction. 2. Family life—New York (State)—Fiction. 3. Orphans—Fiction. 4. World War, 1939–1945—Fiction. 5. Cooking—Fiction. 6. Missing in action—Fiction. 7. Ghosts—Fiction. 8. New York (State)—History—20th century—Fiction.) I. Title.
PZ7.G3626Gh 2013
[Fic]—dc23   2012016631

The text of this book is set in 12-point Berling.
Book design by Trish Parcell

Printed in the United States of America

10 9 8 7 6 5 4 3 2 1

First Edition

To Patricia Johanna O'Meara,
my granddaughter,
with love

AFTER . . .

⤳

Just a couple of dreams? Is that what you think? That all of it would have happened without her?

You think I would have gotten myself to Brooklyn, and brought Theresa with me?

Would I have found Coney Island, with the sand like silk under my feet? The waves roaring in my ears? The taste of salt in my mouth?

What about the bakery?

The bakery!

All right. Maybe.

But what about Elise and her story?

Yes, most of all, finding Elise, her hair escaping from her bun, her arms around me?

Could I have done all that alone? I don't think so.

If you don't believe in ghosts or voices that come out of almost nowhere, there's probably no sense in reading what I have to say.

Then again, you might be surprised.

Chapter 1

જી

"I'll be right there, Rob," I called.

Did my brother hear me?

He was in the kitchen chopping onions, the knife going a mile a minute. WJZ Radio was blasting news to anyone who wanted to listen. It was all about the war in the Pacific. I didn't want to think about it.

I clumped into his boots. They were huge and much too heavy, but who knew where mine were? From my window, I'd seen a flower in the swampy pond at the end of our garden, a buttery yellow lily.

Amazing. It was late for flowers, almost winter. It might be close enough to pick. I was going to find out.

I took the path out back, stamped through the

weeds, then stepped into the water, sliding a little. Mud and old leaves oozed up around my feet. From the corner of my eye, I saw something floating around on the other side of the pond.

My hat?

My old Sunday hat, the blue ribbons trailing behind, completely bedraggled!

How did it get there?

I couldn't be bothered about that right now. It was the flower I was after.

I sloshed in a little farther. The water was freezing; I could feel it right through Rob's boots. Then the mud covered the boots. I couldn't take another step.

It reminded me of something I'd seen in the movies: a girl sinking to her nose in quicksand. "Arghh," I whispered, just the way she had.

One day I'd be a movie star. I'd be grown up, and the war would be over. Or I'd be a famous chef, wearing a tall white hat, with movie stars crowding into my restaurant.

"Hey, Rob!" I yelled toward the house. "I'm stuck in here."

He waved from the kitchen window, the chopping knife raised in his hand. "On my way, Jayna," he yelled back.

I waited, paddling my hands in the icy water, wiggling my toes in his boots. The pond was filling in with old leaves and branches; the stream that fed it was no more than a trickle. Rob had said it wouldn't be a pond much longer, just a patch of mud.

A couple of insects skated across the water and a blue heron high-stepped around the reeds. The turtle we called Theresa was in the middle of the pond, teetering on a thin branch that had broken off from the willow tree. Her shell was thick and curved, a beautiful brown and gold.

What would she do when her pond turned into a patch of mud? She'd have to take her dinner-plate-sized self and lumber off to find a new place.

What about me, when Rob left next week? He wouldn't be coming home from the naval base every night. He'd be halfway around the world on a destroyer, fighting in the war I didn't want to think about.

Theresa blinked with heavy lids. Maybe she was wondering about me, a skinny creature who fed her dried bugs and raw hamburger meat every day, a creature with sudden tears in her eyes.

I brushed at my face with two muddy fingers. *Think about being a movie star. Rich and famous. Think about that tall chef's hat plunked over my ginger hair.*

Rob came across the yard and swung me out of the brackish water, leaving one boot stuck in the muck. My brother, Rob, nine years older than me, was big and bulky because he loved to cook and, even more, to eat anything he cooked! He was great at it: burgers and fries, steak and baked potatoes, lemon meringue pie and apple turnovers.

No wonder he was a cook in the navy. And now he'd be on a destroyer, the *Muldoon*, cooking for the sailors.

Do not waste one minute thinking about the Muldoon. *Not even one second.*

Rob looked at my muddy self. "So why were you trying to take a bath in the pond?"

I pointed to the yellow flower.

"You'd never reach that flower in a million years."

"It was almost my last chance," I said. "When you leave, I'll be halfway across town, staying with Celine."

Another thing not to think about! Celine, our landlady, would drive me out of my mind.

"Bad enough we have to have dinner with her every other minute," I told Rob. "Worse that she'll take care of me full-time." He opened his mouth to say something, but I rushed on. "Don't even say her name. I don't want to think about Celine tapping around on Cuban heels, her hairpiece looped over one eye, telling me to act like a lady."

"Poor Celine." Rob leaned back against the scrawny willow tree. "Actually, she's been a good friend and a good landlady."

I wanted to say, *Don't go.* I wanted to throw my arms

around him and say, *We just made ourselves into a family a year ago.*

Not much of a family, only two people, but still so much better than before. I closed my eyes, remembering the day he'd come for me.

"Why don't you wait?" Mrs. Alman, the foster woman, had said.

"Not even a second." Rob had smiled at both of us. "No more Sunday visits. I'm old enough now, legal."

I'd run down the path with him, looking back for a second to wave goodbye to Mrs. Alman, and in the car, the two of us had laughed with tears in our eyes.

"If only you didn't have to go," I said now. "Suppose you get killed?"

He shook his head. "Wait a minute, Gingersnap."

My mother's nickname for me.

Before I knew it, he'd sloshed into the water that didn't even reach his knees and took three enormous steps toward the flower. He reached out with one hand, almost touching it.

I held my breath as the flower bobbed just out of reach.

"Yeow." He slid into the mud, water spraying onto the bank, then came up, holding a stone in his raised hand. "No flower today, but this is for you, the world's best soup maker. Now you can make stone soup."

I grinned. I could do anything with a pot of

vegetables, a little stock, a chunk or two of meat, and a pinch of basil or oregano.

The stone just fit in my hand. As I looked down at it, I could imagine a face: indentations that were almost eyes, a small curved nose.

"With that little turned-up nose, it almost looks like you," Rob said.

"A funny face," I said.

"That's what makes it great. Imagine, it's been around forever, rolling down from a mountain or coming up from under the sea. She might bring us luck, Jayna, this funny stone girl."

"We need luck." I slipped the stone into my pocket, and we went up to the house. I hopped, holding my bare foot up in the cold air. I held the sleeve of his wet jacket with two wet fingers.

"That water is really freezing," he said, then stopped, frowning. "I forgot. Celine is coming to dinner."

"I should have drowned myself," I said.

"Instead of my boot."

"You wasted a perfectly good night inviting her," I said. "*Lux Theater* is on the radio at nine o'clock. I was going to curl up and listen. . . ."

"And I ruined a perfectly good jacket trying to get that flower for you. But maybe Celine will be gone by nine. Besides, I've made a perfectly good dinner. And afterward, we'll get everything settled with her."

That Celine.

I didn't stop in the kitchen. I went down the hall toward the bathroom to sit on the edge of the tub, washing off my foot, thinking what it would be like here in North River without Rob. I was used to him coming home from the base every night and being free most weekends. That was why we'd chosen to live in North River, after all—to be together while he trained. I was used to cooking with him, laughing with him, hiking up the hills outside town with him.

When would the war ever be over?

Chapter 2

I went into the kitchen and set the table for the three of us, giving Celine the plate with the chip on the edge.

Rob thickened the gravy, stirring in cornstarch with rosemary and garlic, while I made lemon icing, eating a spoonful as I spread it over the graham-cracker cake he'd made.

He glanced across at me. "The cake won't be as good as usual. Only one egg, and lard. It's all because of the war. . . ."

He didn't have to finish. Food was rationed, and we couldn't always get eggs or butter. How hard it was to find everything we needed. Still, the dinner was going to be fine, just as Rob had promised.

News came from the small white radio on the shelf, hints of convoys moving toward the islands off Japan. That was why Rob was leaving the base and heading to California, where he'd board the *Muldoon*.

He saw my worried face. "She's a great ship. Fast and sure in the water."

I held up my hand. "Don't."

He nodded and started our game: what we'd do when the war was over and he came home.

When, I told myself. Not *if*.

"We'll pack our bags and leave North River," he began.

"Bringing all your recipe books," I said.

He nodded. "We'll go to Brooklyn."

I didn't know Brooklyn. I knew only those towns near North River where I'd lived in foster homes before Rob rescued me.

"We'll open a restaurant," I said. "You can cook all day."

"And you'll make soup."

Celine knocked at the door and pattered in, her small feet on a pillow body, her hairpiece askew. What was underneath that nest?

She looked around as always, trying to see how we kept the house.

A mess.

We went to the table and Rob brought in the steaming dishes. Never mind the dust and the piles of books and sweaters on the couch; there wasn't one thing wrong with the cooking.

Without thinking, I rested my arms on the table.

"Your elbows will turn into camels' heels if you keep leaning on them like that," Celine said.

I opened my mouth to say something mean, but Rob winked at me, so I closed it.

Celine knew it. "Closed teeth are fences against bad words." She glanced up at the ceiling, her mouth filled with lamb. Her hairpiece slid lower as she chewed. How could she see?

She started in on the news, the war, and Rob's leaving. "Dangerous," she said.

As if we didn't know it. Rob and I looked at each other, and suddenly it was hard not to laugh. Quickly I bent my head over my plate.

Celine hadn't noticed. "But don't worry," she went on. "Think of that pilot, Eddie Rickenbacker, and his crew, who were on rafts in the Pacific for weeks, starving." She shook her head, her hairpiece quivering, as she helped herself to half the bowl of carrots.

"A seagull landed on his hat," Rob said calmly. "It was enough food to get them through."

"Our fleet is massing for a huge attack in the Pacific," Celine said, her mouth full. "Everyone knows that."

Take a few deep breaths.

"So I'll keep Jayna," she went on. "I certainly will. I'm not doing it for money. It's for the good of the country."

"I'll send you almost everything I make," Rob said.

Celine was coughing now, choking on the pound of carrots she'd crowded into her mouth.

Some manners.

Rob poured a glass of water for her. In science class this morning, Mrs. Murtha had said, "Let's think about water. If you drop a ball into a bowl, the water has to move away to make room for it."

"Huh," Joseph had said in his seat behind me.

Mrs. Murtha had ignored him. "When a ship enters the ocean, the same thing happens. The water has to make room for it. That's called *displacement*."

"Everyone's displaced because of the war," a voice whispered behind me.

Joseph? Diane?

No.

The whisper came again. "Pushed away from my misty silver lake, peace gone. I'll have to spend my days here."

I turned around. I saw . . .

Something? Someone? A lock of ginger hair, almost like mine, that faded into nothing.

Mrs. Murtha was staring at me.

Had I fallen asleep?

Now I glanced across the dinner table at Rob.

13

He was going to be displaced, taken away from North River, away from me. I'd be displaced into Celine's house up on the hill.

I stared at my plate for the rest of the meal. I barely finished the lamb and hardly tasted the graham-cracker cake with the icing I loved.

At last Celine put on her hat. "I have to be home before it gets really dark. Who knows? Robbers and thieves may be hiding. . . ." Her voice trailed off as she opened our front door.

We watched her hurry down the street. "As if a robber would dare go near her," Rob said, laughter in his voice.

We went back into the kitchen to cut ourselves huge slices of cake. Celine was gone! We could eat in peace.

Rob began to talk about the war. "My ship will steam into the South Pacific," he said. "It will be part of a huge convoy to take the islands from the Japanese: Iwo Jima, Okinawa, then Honshu, Hokkaido. . . ."

Names that sounded strange to my ears. Names I didn't want to hear.

The big radio was on in the living room and *Lux Theater* was beginning. "Don't spoil the cake. Don't spoil *Lux*." I hesitated. "Suppose your ship is blown up."

"You sound like Celine with her robbers and thieves." He held up his hand. "The *Muldoon*'s a powerful ship. She cuts through the water like the blade of a knife."

"What will happen to me if . . ." I couldn't finish.

He came around to my side of the table and put his large hands on my shoulders. "You are tough, Jayna. You are strong. I've seen that over and over. You're like our mother. You'll always know what to do."

Not true, I wanted to say. Not at all true. But still, how wonderful it was to be compared to the mother I never knew.

"So think that," Rob said. "Jayna the strong. Jayna the brave."

"Yes, think that," a voice whispered.

I turned, but no one was there.

xxx

Stone Soup

INGREDIENTS

An empty pot

A couple cups of water

A funny stone girl

A carrot from Celine

A bay leaf from Rob

A hunk of meat from John the butcher

WHAT TO DO

Mix, cook, and pour into a soup bowl.

Careful of your teeth on the stone.

xxxxxxxxxxxxxxxxxxxxxxxxxxxxxxxxxxxxxxxxxxxxxxxxxxx

Chapter 3

From my window the next morning, I watched the sun turn the pond to gold. Leaves drifted along on the water; only a few were left on the trees.

I flew down to the water's edge, spotted Theresa, and sprinkled dried insects from the turtle food box for her to snap at.

Then I leaned against the yellow willow tree. Last night, I couldn't concentrate on *Lux Theater* after all. I kept thinking of our mother and father, who had died long ago. I'd never seen their pictures. I couldn't imagine what they looked like, even though I tried.

I pretended to change my mother's hair from long to short, her lips pink to red, her dresses long to short, just the way I'd drawn in my coloring books. I'd made my father tall, looking like Rob, sometimes with a mustache, sometimes not.

I'd whisper their names, Claude and Marie Louise, Father and Mother, both gone in a car accident. I tried to imagine what life would be like if they hadn't been in that car. We'd listen to *Lux Theater* together on Monday nights or the *Shadow* on Sundays. Sometimes we'd go to the movies. And every night at bedtime, we'd call out *I love you* to each other.

After *Lux*, I'd stared across at Rob. He had a tiny dab of icing on the edge of his mouth; his crew cut was brushed up dark and stiff.

"What?" Rob asked.

"I want to know more about our mother and father."

I thought of living in those foster homes, not far from North River. Rob had lived in another home nearby. All those years, he'd come to see me on Sundays. I'd asked him the same question every time.

"She wore a blue ring on her finger," he'd say, or "She had curly hair like yours. She called you Gingersnap."

Rob looked at the silent radio. "Sometimes she sang French songs. Her parents were French."

That was new. Why hadn't I known that?

"She loved to cook. Dough was always rising in the kitchen."

I did know that. I waved my hand. "What about our father?"

"He laughed a lot, a big laugh." Rob raised his shoulders. "He went to work in the city."

"What else?"

He shook his head. "I was always playing ball. I didn't pay attention. I'll try to think."

He always said that. The story of our parents came out in dribs and drabs.

Rob frowned a little. "I do remember something."

I held my breath.

"There's a box on top of my closet. At least, I think there is, somewhere in back. It has my baseball glove. . . ."

"Please," I said, grinning. "Am I interested in your baseball glove?"

He grinned back. "There are a few pictures and a recipe book. The book's in French—you can't read a word. But there's something about a bakery." He raised his shoulders. "Something about a grandmother. I meant to check it out after I saw it again last year, but I've been so busy here and at the base."

I nodded.

"When I come home," he said, "we'll look at it together."

On the other side of the pond, I saw my old Sunday hat again, most of it under the surface of the water; I couldn't see the blue ribbons anymore. Still, I walked toward it, around the other side of the pond.

Rob would leave, and I'd be alone. I whispered the

19

words that meant a family. I used to say them every night: cousins, aunts, uncles, grandfather, loving the sounds on my tongue. I'd make them up: Cousin Eleanor, Aunt Elaine, Grandpa.

One Sunday I'd told Rob that. "I used to do the same thing," he said. "Uncle John, Cousin Pete."

The hat was almost in my reach, the way the yellow flower had been. I moved closer and was just able to run my fingers over the sodden crown.

"Don't bother," a voice said. "It's a terrible mess."

I spun around. Who could that possibly be? Was it coming from the top of the shed? A soft voice, a high voice. A small stone rattled its way down from the roof.

I saw a pair of feet. Whoever it was wore one of my yellow striped socks and the green one with the hole in the toe.

Who was it?

The hat teetered on the edge of the little waterfall, dragging the blue ribbons behind it, and disappeared over the edge.

"Too late anyway," the voice said. "Just let it go, Jayna."

I stood on tiptoe to see who was up there, but even the feet were gone now.

I had to be dreaming. There'd been too much to worry about.

"Yes," the voice said. "Too much all at once, I know. Even for me."

Who was reading my mind?

The voice went on. "You can't imagine what's in store for you, but at least I'll be there, helping you find what you need."

I took a quick breath. Then I ran. Around the pond. Through the yard. And into the house.

I locked the kitchen door behind me, circled Rob's duffel bag in the hall, and went up to my room.

"Too much," I whispered. I could hear Rob in the bathroom, fixing a leak, whistling. What was that song?

"We'll Meet Again."

Should I tell him about that voice?

One Sunday, when I was five, he'd come for his usual visit. "Get me out of here," I'd said. "There's a lizard living under my bed. A blue one."

He'd nodded seriously, as if he believed every word.

He'd nod seriously this time, too.

But how could he believe in a ghost?

Was it a ghost?

Someone with a high voice? Someone who wore my socks and ruined my hat?

How could he possibly believe that? I could hardly believe it myself.

I wasn't going to think about it one more minute. I marched into the kitchen and pulled out the old pot. I'd make soup instead.

XXX

Don't-Think-About-It Soup

INGREDIENTS

Piles of onions chopped up (Stick parsley in your mouth so you don't cry.)

Some meat stock (old beef bones, carrots, thyme, and lots of water simmered for an hour)

Salt and pepper, of course

Bread and oleo

WHAT TO DO

Cut some bread into cubes.

Melt oleo in the pot.

Salt the onions and cook them gently.

Add the stock.

Cook that, too.

Toast that bread.

Drop it on top of the soup.

See, you've forgotten to think.

XXXXXXXXXXXXXXXXXXXXXXXXXXXXXXXXXXXXXXXXXXXXXXXXXXX

Chapter 4

The days passed so slowly they might have been glued together. I scuffed through the dry fall leaves and wrote to Rob on Thanksgiving: *Taught Celine how to make stuffing for the turkey. She made the mashed potatoes. I dropped a precious egg on the floor. Eek! Thank goodness it wasn't her almost-genuine Ming vase . . . but she acted as if it were just as bad. Fingers crossed. When the war is over, we'll have dozens of eggs.*

Christmas came, with knitted socks to Celine from me and a book on manners to me from her.

Four letters arrived from Rob in one swoop. One told of seasickness, one of frying Spam and doctoring up cans of sodden vegetables, another about seeing phosphorous in the rolling water, glints of green that were magical to watch.

Lincoln's birthday came next. I walked along the street with my head back, staring up at the trees, searching for signs of spring. Nothing yet, but I did get a lump on my forehead from careening into an oak tree.

Sometimes I wondered about the voice. I hadn't heard it since Rob had left, months ago.

The day he left: duffel bag over his shoulder, the two of us waiting for his train. It came in with a whoosh of air, and I was determined not to cry.

Once inside, he'd pulled up the window. "I'll be back!" he yelled.

"Anchors aweigh!" I yelled after him, waving until the tracks turned at the end of town and the train was gone.

⌒

Celine bought me a hat for Easter Sunday. Imagine, my first veil. It had little blue dots, and I kept blowing at it all through church to get it out of my eyes. I loved it!

Sometimes Celine surprised me.

We listened to the radio when we ate lunch. The

announcer called the first day of Operation Iceberg "Love Day." "Iwo Jima has fallen, with a terrible loss of lives on both sides," he said in that deep radio voice. "Twelve thousand ships and a half million men are steaming toward Okinawa, an island seventy miles long, ten miles wide. . . ."

He kept talking, but all I heard was *twelve thousand ships*. Where was the *Muldoon* in this? Where was Rob?

Later that afternoon, I walked over to our house with the blue roof. I checked the pond. Yes, Theresa had climbed out of the muddy winter bottom; she was sunning herself on the other side of the pond.

I went up to the back door, leaning forward to pull out the key that was looped around my neck, and stepped into the kitchen.

A calendar hung on the wall so I could mark off the days. It was the first of April.

What made me go upstairs? I hadn't been in my bedroom since the day I'd moved into Celine's. But I walked through the living room, running my fingers over the dusty end tables, and went up the stairs.

My room was a mess, the closet door and dresser drawers open, a pile of socks on the floor.

Had I left it that way?

"Sorry," the voice said. "I was trying on a few things. Your jacket with the silver buttons just fit."

My heart thumped, its beat somewhere in my throat.

I couldn't run. I could see her feet, on tiptoes in the hall. I'd have to pass her to get to the stairs.

"I'm back," she said.

"I see that." I could hear the tremor in my voice, but I tried to sound calm; I tried to sound as if I saw ten polished toes every day, with only a hint of the rest of her. "You're wearing my nail polish."

"Yes, Pink Strawberry, very nice." Her hand rested on the edge of the door. Her fingernails were polished, too, but they were bitten way down. Mine were growing at last. Celine was after me every time she saw my hand go to my mouth.

"Who are you?" I asked.

"I'm trying to figure that out, but don't worry, I'm harmless."

I took a step back. I could always jump out the window onto the porch over the kitchen.

"I wouldn't do that," the voice said. "I tried it before. It's a nasty fall if you miss."

"I don't believe in ghosts," I muttered.

"I don't, either. But that's what I am. . . . At least, I think so."

"But who were you?"

She sighed. "I don't remember. How about that queen?" She snapped her bitten fingers. "Mary, the Scottish one?"

I shivered. "Her head was chopped off."

"No," she said. "Definitely not."

I was talking to ten fingers, ten toes. How could that be?

"There was Marie Antoinette," she went on. "But she had a problem with her head, too."

Ridiculous.

"Do you like the name Cleo?" she asked.

I shook my head. "It sounds like a fish."

"No, I'm not a fish, either." She sounded annoyed. "But heads rolling and fish swimming are not what I'm about right this minute. You can call me Ghost, or Voice." She waved her hand. "Whatever you like. We're going to spend a lot of time together." I saw a strand of reddish hair looped over a collar. "Remember that when Stuart comes. It will help."

What was she talking about? Did I even know a Stuart?

I brushed past her and went down the stairs. It wasn't enough that I was living with Celine, waiting for mail from Rob that rarely came. Now I had to deal with a ghost who was wearing my nail polish.

I heard the clock chime as I passed the living room. Four-thirty. Celine, back in her kitchen working on a leathery ham, would have an absolute fit, wondering what I was up to.

"Wait," the voice said behind me. "You have to listen. Stuart will be coming."

I didn't turn toward her. It was much easier to look out the window, to pretend she wasn't there. I paused, then went out the door and walked up the street. I had to pass the Western Union office, closed and dark on Easter Sunday.

I stopped short. Stuart. The old man who sat behind the desk, the one who rode his bicycle when he delivered telegrams that told of men missing or killed in action.

Chapter 5

Every day there was news about the war in the Pacific. A week after Easter, a huge battleship, the *Yamoto*, had been hit and sunk. I kept thinking about what the radio announcer had said: "The Japanese sailors had just enough fuel to take them from their mainland to Okinawa, and it had been for nothing."

Displaced.

All that month we heard about kamikaze planes diving into destroyers and battleships.

Please not Rob's ship, not the Muldoon.

Mrs. Murtha drew arrows on the blackboard, showing those planes diving and looping, exploding into our ships. One morning, with tears in her eyes, she told us that our president had died, and there would be a new president, a man named Harry Truman.

True man. The sound of it was hopeful. I made myself think about that.

May began; the sun grew warmer every day. "Wednesday afternoon," Celine told me after school one day. "So much to do. Groceries from Milton's, meat from John's."

"I'll go . . . ," I said

"You'll get it all wrong," she said. "I'll go. You might wash the breakfast dishes instead, and dust the living room."

I nodded. From her kitchen window I could see all the way down the hill, almost to the telegraph office. The sidewalks were dotted with sycamore trees, their leaves beginning to unfurl, and three or four kids were playing Giant Steps in the street.

"Are you listening to me, Jayna?" Celine asked, her hairpiece sliding over one eye.

"Sorry." I had to stop thinking about what the ghost had said about Stuart. Was the ghost real or only something I'd made up?

"When you dust, be careful of the almost-genuine Ming vase in the hall," Celine said. "I've had it for years." She pushed the hairpiece up on her freckled forehead.

I'd heard about that vase at least a dozen times.

Celine went down the street, her shopping bag on

her arm, her snood covering her hair, as I stacked the dishes in the sink and blasted the water over them.

More kids were outside now. They darted back and forth in the street, one taking banana steps, another taking baby steps. "May I?" one of them yelled as another sneaked forward. I watched them while I dried the dishes and dusted the tables, making a wide circle around that vase.

I sat down to write to Rob. "If you don't write, you're wrong," Kate Smith said on the radio every day. I tried, but there was so little to say.

I glanced out the window again. Celine was coming back, laboring up the hill, carrying a knobby bag.

Stuart was behind her, his skinny legs pumping the bicycle wheels. His hand went to the bell on the front, a telegram in his fist. Celine turned. The two of them leaned toward each other, Stuart doing the talking.

Celine's hand went to her mouth, and they both looked up the hill toward me.

That was all I saw.

That was all I needed to see.

I ran through the hall toward the stairs, knocking over the almost-genuine Ming vase, hearing it shatter into a hundred pieces. I stopped to lock the front door so Stuart couldn't give me that telegram.

My feet clattered up the stairs, the bedroom door banged shut behind me, and I slammed into the closet, sinking down in the middle of Celine's clothes, smelling the camphor balls she'd strewn around to protect against the moths.

The telegram.

Did they all begin the same? *We regret to inform you . . .*

That meant Rob.

Would they regret that something had happened to him?

His ship: *a destroyer fast and sure, cutting through the waves.* But the Pacific Ocean was huge and dark. It was filled with sharks gliding under the surface, while overhead, fighter planes were diving, diving. . . .

While I was wearing a hat with a veil, was Rob in the mess hall? Still all right? Not guessing what was going to happen? And while I was studying the products of New York State in school, had the water covered the deck and flooded down the stairs toward him?

Or had there been an explosion? Had he heard the sound of it, that terrible roar?

My dear Rob, big and bulky, who loved to cook, who loved to eat.

Rob, my brother.

Rob, who was all I had.

Stuart was knocking. It hadn't done any good for me to lock the door. Celine had a key. Of course she did. Sometimes she left it in the Ming vase. I remembered the sound of the metal dropping against the china.

No more.

No more Ming vase.

No more Rob?

They were in the house.

I pictured them stepping over the shards of the vase. "Jayna, where are you?" Celine called, her voice trembling.

I buried my head in a long silky gray dress with a scalloped hem. I couldn't imagine that Celine had ever worn something like that.

She was coming up the stairs. Then, through the small crack of light, I saw her standing in the doorway. "Jayna?"

My mouth was pressed against that silky dress, the smell of camphor so strong I could feel it burning my nostrils and my throat.

Celine took a few steps across the room and opened the closet door. "You have to come out." She was breathless. "Stuart is here from the telegraph office. He has a telegram. It's for you."

She had to know what it said, but I couldn't open my mouth to tell her that.

"Don't worry about the vase," she said.

The vase?

"It was only almost genuine. It wasn't important, after all."

Celine being kind. It made it all worse somehow.

I stood up, rattling the hangers; the dress slid to the floor in a puddle of gray.

I went past her down the stairs to the hall, where Stuart was standing in the midst of broken china.

"I'm sorry, Jayna," he said, and handed me the beige envelope.

I ripped it open. Yes, someone was regretting about Rob. He was missing, but they'd let me know further details as soon as they were available.

Just words, each one pasted on the telegram paper. Not even kind words.

Stuart ran his hand over his bald head; then he was gone.

Celine came down the stairs toward me, her arms out. She held me against her pillow body, both of us rocking back and forth.

Celine.

It was hard to believe.

I stepped back and shrugged into my jacket, which was on the stair post.

"Let's have tea," she said. "A nice cup of tea always helps."

"I have to go home," I said.

"But there's no one there."

No one.

I listened. Did the voice say, "He's still alive?"

But it was only the sound of my own footsteps going down the street.

Chapter 6

I went back to the pond, to Theresa, who was swimming lazily with only her head and her dark eyes above the water.

What was I going to do?

How long would it take Celine to realize that she might have me there forever?

I'd have to live with her.

It was unthinkable.

Theresa lumbered up on the other side of the pond, a smear of mud across her beautiful golden brown shell.

I could picture what might have happened: A small, dark speck in the sky, a plane coming closer. I could almost hear it diving, the noise of it high, whining, sailors looking up, firing. The plane hits the deck with a tremendous explosion. A ball of fire rises, spreads, sparks. . . .

"Stop," the voice said from behind the willow tree. "That doesn't do any good."

"Do you think he's alive?"

She sighed. "I don't know."

Did I see her shake her head?

I stood up and brushed dirt off my socks. Then I went up to the house. I wandered around downstairs: the kitchen where we'd had dinner, the living room with the big radio.

I started up the stairs.

"Yes," said the voice. "You know where you're going."

I didn't pay attention to her. I wandered in and out of my bedroom, stepping over a slipper, then headed down the hall to Rob's room.

"The closet," she said.

I closed my eyes. "There's a box," he'd said. "My baseball glove."

I opened the closet door. Sneakers and a coat. A jacket.

"On the shelf," she said.

I dragged a chair over and stood up, pushing aside his hats. A couple of books clunked down to the floor, just missing my foot.

36

I reached for the box, able to touch it with one finger, and edged it toward me, steadying it with my other hand. It came slowly and then teetered on the edge of the shelf. I grabbed it and slid off the chair.

"Now we're getting somewhere," said the voice.

I slid it open. A peacock feather lay across the top. Just under it was a picture of a man and a woman who had to be my father and mother. My mother wore a hat with a feather—the peacock feather, of course—and my father looked down at her, smiling with even white teeth under his mustache.

Rob stood next to them, a little boy. He looked so much the way he did now, except that his hair was longer then.

I held the picture to my face and cried for my parents, who were really strangers, and for Rob, who was so far away, who might not even be alive.

"Ah, no," the voice said. "Don't do that."

I wiped my eyes on my sleeve and went through the rest of the box. I patted the baseball glove, tried on a pair of woolen mittens that must have been Rob's, and looked at the picture of a baby in lace. The baby was probably me, certainly not very pretty.

"She has a lot of curls," the voice said, and I almost smiled. That was about the best you could say about that baby.

At the bottom of the box was a book. I pulled it out,

running my hands over the faded blue cover; it was soft under my fingers. I opened it, looking down at the handwritten recipes.

At first the words were large and loopy, but by the middle of the book the letters were smaller, firmer. I could picture the writer growing older. I couldn't read a word. It was all in French.

Sometimes she sang French songs.

My mother's recipe book?

What had Rob said? A bakery? A grandmother?

So long ago, did it even matter?

But there was an address inside the cover—Carey Street, Brooklyn, New York—and a name—Elise Martin. I went through the pages. Somewhere in the middle was an old black-and-white photo. It showed a girl with braids wrapped around her head, not smiling, but squinting into the camera. I didn't think it was my mother, but who was it?

I liked her face, her serious eyes staring out at me.

I held the photo to the light. She was standing in front of a bakery. I held the photo one way and then another. A striped awning shaded the shop window. A name was written above the scallops. I could only just make it out, but I couldn't believe what I saw.

I went down to the kitchen, opening one drawer after another, searching for the magnifying glass. I finally put my hand on it, in with rolled-up balls of string and can openers.

I hurried upstairs again and took the picture to the windowsill. There it was, the name stretched out across the awning: GINGERSNAP.

"A coincidence," I said aloud.

"No," the voice said. "I don't think so."

I sat back on my heels. The time was going. Celine would be waiting.

Gingersnap!

"You're going to Brooklyn," the voice said. "We'll find that bakery, and a family for you."

"It may not even be there anymore," I said.

"Yes, it is."

I shook my head. "I can't do that."

"I'll be with you."

I kept shaking my head, but I didn't want to go up the hill to Celine's. I wanted to . . .

"Go to Brooklyn," the voice said. "I think it's in Mexico, or Canada. People wear leis."

What nonsense, Celine would have said. "It's only a few hours away."

Did I see her smile? Was she teasing me? "Well, there we are," she said. "Ready to go."

I went back to Celine's. Of course, I wasn't ready to go. I wasn't ready to do anything. I let myself in the door and heard Celine talking on the phone.

"I can't come," she was saying. "I have to be here for Jayna. It sounds like a wonderful trip. . . ." Her voice trailed off. "Someday I'll have my life back."

Yes. That was what I wanted, too. I remembered Rob's hands on my shoulders. *Jayna the strong; Jayna the brave.* And somehow, as impossible as it seemed, I was going to Brooklyn. Maybe I'd find the bakery with my name. I'd find the woman with her hair in braids.

"Yes," the voice said.

Chapter 7

The next day I went back to our house, to plan, to think, to decide. Could I really do this?

I had money. Rob had left me piles of it to get through until he got home. So that was all right. But skipping school? That was a little scary, but so was all of it.

I went into my closet and pulled out a few things. I packed them into my old suitcase.

"Put the blue book in your pocket," the voice said behind me.

"There's room in my suitcase."

"You're going to lose that suitcase."

"I am not." I was angry now, angry at everything. I put the book in a nest of socks in the case and heard the voice sigh.

"You do a lot of sighing," I said.

"That's what ghosts are supposed to do. I've been practicing."

I paid no attention; I stood there, turning slowly. What else did I need?

"Theresa," the voice said.

Theresa! That was impossible.

I looked over my shoulder to glimpse a pointed nose, a strand of hair across an apple-round cheek, teeth crowded together, almost like mine.

Then nothing was there.

I crossed my hands over my shoulders, chilled. I glanced out the window. How could I leave Theresa to dry up in that swampy pond?

"You can't," she said.

I went back down the hall to the spare room. I remembered seeing a carrying case, probably for a cat. But it would have to do.

*

I went back to Celine's house for one more night.

Where was Rob?

Was he just gone?

Celine met me at the door. "Are you all right?" she

42

asked. Maybe she was still thinking about her phone call and wanting her life back.

I nodded. Still she looked worried.

"I'll make soup," I said.

"Use the stove? Suppose you burn yourself? Suppose you spill . . ."

"I told you," the voice whispered. "We have to get out of here. We have to go to Brooklyn."

I walked into the kitchen and opened Celine's icebox. It was packed with food, jams and jellies, carrots, and a wedge of cheese. I moved things around, pulling things out.

Behind me Celine pattered around, sighing almost as the ghost had sighed, wondering, I guess, what she was ever going to do with me in her life.

I wanted to say, *I'm leaving. I'm going to Brooklyn. I'm going to find a bakery.* Of course, I didn't say that, but I felt a small thread of . . . almost happiness.

"Yes," I heard the ghost say. Was she humming that French nursery rhyme "Frère Jacques"?

XX

Feel-Better Vegetable Soup

INGREDIENTS

Whatever is in the icebox. Maybe:

Carrots

A green pepper

An onion

String beans or peas

Some of that meat stock

And a fistful of rice

WHAT TO DO

Throw it all in and let it simmer. You don't have to pay much attention. Stop cooking when you get sick of waiting.

Breathe it in as you sip. Think of the steam, the saltiness, the warmth.

XXXXXXXXXXXXXXXXXXXXXXXXXXXXXXXXXXXXXXXXXXXXXXXXXXXX

Chapter 8

I left Celine's house as soon as it was light, tiptoe-ing down the stairs, past the empty table where the almost-genuine Ming vase had stood. A small shard lay on the wooden floor.

For the first time, I felt sorry for Celine, and sorry about the vase.

I stopped at our house, then went out the door with my suitcase in one hand and Theresa in her case in the other. All of it was heavier than I'd realized. At the last minute I'd packed my reader, *Children of the World*, and my geography book, which had a picture of New York State with its major products on the front cover.

I patted my pocket; a box of dried food for Theresa

was there, and deep inside was the funny little stone girl Rob had found for me. It made him seem closer, and maybe it would bring me luck.

Remember that day at the pond, I told myself. *Don't think about enemy planes. Don't think about orange flames and explosions.*

Celine slept late every morning. I had scribbled a note to her about visiting relatives. Would she believe it? At the bottom of the page, I'd written, *Someday I'll buy you another almost-genuine Ming vase. Please have your life back.*

I turned left toward town, already worn out. I'd been awake in the middle of the night, tears on my cheeks, staring up at the ceiling. My eyes were swollen, and it was hard to think. I kept looking over my shoulder, but there was no one on the street, not a teacher, not Breslin the cop, not my friend Diane, who bicycled to school every morning.

The walk to Rosemont for the bus was far, but it was safe. No one would see that I wasn't on my way to school. ·

I turned right and walked along Front Street to the end of town. I'd have to cross the highway. I stood there, looking down at the embankment.

How steep it was!

I left Theresa in her case on top, and I began to slide with my suitcase.

Gravel scraped my wrists, tore the edge of my purse,

and dented the suitcase. I tumbled to a stop at the bottom, full of dust, and glanced back up. My heels had made indentations all the way down, like a small pair of twisted roads.

I left everything behind a large rock and went back for Theresa. I looked at her in the cat case, but as always, she was calm, blinking her heavy lids, staring at me. "We're all right," I whispered.

Was it really true?

A trailer truck hurtled by with its horn blaring as I zigzagged to the other side of the highway. For a moment, I sat at the edge. Both my elbows were skinned, and there was a cut on my ankle.

A school bus passed, and a boy I'd never seen before looked out the window at me, surprised.

He wouldn't know Celine. She'd never find out he'd seen me sitting at the edge of the road.

I slung my purse over my shoulder, picked up the cases, and followed the river south. The sound of bubbling water cascading over the rocks was cooling, but the walk was endless; my feet burned.

I remembered reading about a woman who walked forty-three miles every day. I hoped her shoes were better than mine; it wasn't long before blisters rose on the backs of my heels. Still, there was no help for it. I couldn't get the bus in town. People knew I was supposed to be in Mrs. Murtha's room.

I sank down at the edge of the river and bent over to

scoop up water. Not to drink. Rob had taught me better than that. I splashed it on my face and neck and ran my wet hands over my head, patting down my hair, which never wanted to stay straight.

I wanted to take off my shoes and socks. How cool that water would feel on my feet. I'd never get the shoes on again, though.

Don't cry, I told myself.

I stood up and kept going. The sun was over the trees now. I limped, my socks sticking to my raw heels, but the bus stop was right there, two blocks into Rosemont.

The ticket seller punched out a ticket to New York City, yawning, hardly looking at me.

I waited for the bus, slurping down an orange soda and then a second one. I didn't see anyone I knew, only a few soldiers talking and a woman on a bench knitting khaki socks. No one paid attention to a girl climbing onto the bus with scraped hands, a suitcase, and a turtle.

I sat as far back as I could and leaned against the window, watching Rosemont disappear as we pulled onto the highway.

Even though the road was uneven and my head kept bumping against the glass, I slept, dreaming of endless green water with dark shapes underneath.

I missed the rest stop in Montrose and barely woke when the bus driver announced a second stop.

It must have been an hour later when I opened my

eyes. I was just about awake now, dying for something to drink, something to eat, a sandwich, a bag of chips.

All this was like a strange dream: the bus, the woman who sat across from me turning the heel of the sock, the world outside.

And I was taking this long trip to find a bakery with my name.

When I awoke again, I saw a bridge up ahead, a beautiful span with blue-gold water underneath and a tugboat pushing a barge with a white wake of water behind it. The skyline of Manhattan rose in front of me.

But it wasn't Manhattan I was there to see. It was Brooklyn. I'd loved the sound of it, *Brook-lyn*, listening to Rob as we played our game. "Someday we'll go there, you and I. We'll have a restaurant. No one cooks soup like you do."

I was almost there, but I was alone.

Chapter 9

The bus pulled into a gloomy station in Manhattan. I climbed off, blinking in the darkness, to ask my way to the subway. I was amazed at myself. I sounded as if I traveled around every day.

"Where are you going, girlie?" a policeman asked.

"Carey Street," I said. "Brooklyn."

He pointed, and I made my way to an entrance on the corner. Below me, a train whooshed in, loud and grinding. Wind and dust rose up the steps, and people rushed around me, almost throwing themselves down the stairs so they wouldn't miss it.

I didn't know whether to rush, too, but who knew

if it was the right train? I asked the station master and did exactly as he told me. I waited for the next one to come in.

At least, I thought that was what he'd said, but it was all wrong. I got off at a stop marked Coney Island.

"We'll see the ocean," the voice behind me said. Her finger was raised, pointing.

I nodded and crossed the street, my arms aching from carrying Theresa and the suitcase. I climbed up on the boardwalk with sand stinging my eyes and heard music from a merry-go-round: "Pop Goes the Weasel."

Can you imagine? I told Rob in my head. *I'm here in Brooklyn.*

But where was Rob, and was he as hungry as I was now?

Feeling guilty that I could eat, I bought a hot dog, then brought Theresa out of the case for a little exercise. I tossed small chunks of meat into the air, and she stretched her neck to snap at them.

I kept my eye on her as I chewed on the roll. In front of me, waves crashed against the blowing sand. I put Theresa back in her case, talking to her softly. She stared up at me. I was all she had. Not a very satisfying family for a turtle.

Once, I'd tried to figure out how many people loved me. Rob, of course. My mother and father, when they were alive. My teacher Mrs. Murtha had told me that I was a delight. She'd put her hand on the mess of curls on my head. "You're as organized as your hair," she'd said, laughing.

I remembered two goldfish Rob had bought me when we first came to the house. They were buried out near the pond with two little tan stones on top.

"Don't be sad, Jayna," Rob had said as we dug them in. "Goldfish live only a short time, and you gave them a happy life."

I wiped the hot mustard off the edge of my lip and, almost in a daze from the fiery sun, went down the boardwalk steps.

The sand spilled into my shoes, weighing me down. I pulled them off and took a few steps. It was a surprise. The sand was so hot I could hardly bear it against my feet. I ran toward the water, the strap of my purse rubbing against my shoulder, and circled a pair of striped beach umbrellas.

At last, I stood at the water's edge, feeling its icy coldness. The sand underneath my toes was silky, sliding away from my feet; salty waves swirled against my bare legs.

Mrs. Murtha had said once that if all the mountains flattened out, the oceans would cover the land a mile high. I pictured that, the highs covering the lows, until all of it was even, water from the Atlantic meeting the great waves of the Pacific. I saw myself flying over that water, reaching out, searching. . . .

My throat burned. I dipped my fingers into the surf almost as if I could touch him: *Stay alive, Rob, wherever you are.*

I reached into my pocket. My fingers grasped the stone girl. I felt its smoothness. What had Rob said that day? *It's been around forever, rolling down from some mountain, or coming up from under the sea.*

Then I remembered Theresa. I glanced over my shoulder to be sure she was all right in her case. Yes, she was there, but . . .

I shaded my eyes with my hand.

Something was wrong.

Where was my suitcase?

"I knew it," the voice said. "You've lost it. Didn't I tell you?"

"Someone took it. Someone must have . . ."

"It makes no difference. Gone is gone."

In a panic, I ran through the sand, scooping up my shoes, and went up the stairs to look under the bench. I ran up and down on the boardwalk, hardly paying attention to the splinters stabbing into my bare feet. A few people walked along, and two children emptied sand out of their shoes.

No one paid attention to a girl zigzagging along, rushing backward, bending over to look under benches.

It was gone. I went back to Theresa, who slept peacefully in the shade of her case.

I took a couple of breaths and squeezed the water

out of the bottom of my skirt. All I had was what I was wearing.

My hand went to my chest. The money was there under my blouse. But I was a mess. Mustard stains, mud, a spot of orange soda.

What would I do for clothes?

"Don't worry," the voice said.

I couldn't pay attention to her. How could I go to the bakery looking like this? Mrs. Alman, the foster woman, was always talking about street urchins.

That was what I looked like, a street urchin.

"You have money. We'll buy something. A bead necklace for me," the voice said. "I favor pink. I might even be that movie actress, Carole Lombard."

"Killed in a plane crash."

"No good," she said.

It was impossible, all of it. Pink necklaces, no clothes. *Children of the World* was gone, and I'd seen the last of my New York State geography book.

And then the worst.

I'd lost the recipe book. I whispered the address over and over, and then I trudged back to the subway to ask where Carey Street was.

Chapter 10

The houses on Carey Street were tall and brown, with shops on the first floors. An old poster, half torn, flapped on a telephone pole. It showed a man with a beard and a red, white, and blue top hat. He was pointing: *I Want YOU for U.S. Army*.

But what I saw, what I'd been waiting to see, was the bakery. The awning stretched out over the street, with the stripes faded and small rips in the scalloped edges, but my name, Gingersnap, was still there.

Would the woman with braids be there, too? Would she, by some miracle, be my grandmother?

I backed up against a splintery telephone pole. Now that I'd come all this way, what would I say? How could I possibly tell her my mother called me Ginger-snap when I was a baby? How could I say she might be my grandmother, when Rob wasn't sure? I didn't even have the blue recipe book anymore. It was somewhere in the sand, or floating in the water by now.

Underneath the awning was a wrought-iron fence that surrounded a few metal tables. They were empty now except for an old man drinking coffee from a mug. His dog lay on the cracked pavement, half asleep, his head leaning on the man's shoe. It was a white pug, with a skinny little curl of a tail.

What had Rob said not long ago? *We'll have a dog someday, a pair of cats, more fish.*

"Go inside," the voice next to me said softly. "See her now."

I couldn't make myself move. I glanced at a shop across the street. In the window was a frilly dress, as pink as my nail polish. Next to that was a bookshop. A woman with a pageboy haircut hopped around barefoot in the small window. She waved one pudgy hand when she saw me.

A good start. I waved back.

Along the street were empty windows, some on the first floor, others on the second. One had a sign: GONE TO WAR. BACK SOON.

Soon.

"Elise is there," the voice said. "Go ahead, don't be afraid."

I ran my fingers through my hair; my scalp was covered with grains of sand from the wind. I straightened the collar of my blouse and walked up the street, making a wide path around the man's dog.

The dog sprang up and growled. I had to smile. She was small as a cat.

I bent down to see her wrinkled face, and she retreated under the table, looking up at me with worried brown eyes.

"I call her Ella, after Ella Cinders in the comics," the man said, holding a coffee cup in hands that were spattered with age spots. "She's not as brave as she'd like to be."

I liked the look of the man. His hair was thick and white, his mustache a little darker, and his face was gentle as he smiled down at the dog.

I'd tell Rob it was a pug I wanted. White with great dark eyes.

With a tinkle of a small overhead bell, I was inside the bakery. It smelled of ginger and fresh bread. I blinked against the dimness and caught my breath.

The girl I'd seen in the picture was behind the counter. Her braids had become a gray bun on the back of her head. She was much older and bone thin but still beautiful. She had to be Elise, the name on the cover of the recipe book.

Maybe she belonged to me.

I stood back, half listening to the radio behind the

counter as a customer complained. "The last cookies tasted like cardboard."

"We'll meet again," Vera Lynn sang on the radio. *"Don't know where, don't know when . . ."*

I waited, putting the cat carrier on the floor and flexing my fingers, which ached from carrying it. I glanced at the trays inside the glass cases. They held a few loaves of bread with shiny crusts, two or three Danish, and a row of gingersnaps. On a shelf were coffee rings, round and dotted with fruit. A high frosted cake was on top of the counter; small pink roses were looped around the edge.

The customer tapped her foot impatiently as the woman behind the counter slipped a raisin ring into a box, wound string around it, and snapped the end of the string with her fingers.

"I'm bringing it right back," the customer said, "if this one is as bad as the cookies."

Elise leaned forward. "You can't get butter. Eggs are almost as scarce. And sugar is gold. Remember, the government allows only a little bit at a time." She shook her head. "Every time I have to tear a stamp out of my ration book for the grocer, I wonder how I'm going to make the sweet cakes everyone loves."

Something about her voice was unusual. An accent from long ago? I watched her as the impatient woman went out the door and a boy stepped forward. He leaned against the counter. "I thought that raisin ring was pretty good myself," he said. "But what can you expect when the sugar tastes like gold?"

"Ah, Andrew." Elise raised her hands to smooth back her hair. Some of it had escaped her bun and hung in wisps here and there, almost like a halo around her face.

In the picture I'd seen, her eyes had seemed dark, but they were turquoise, so clear and bright they were almost shocking. Did she look like Rob and me? I couldn't tell.

The boy's hair was a mop over his forehead. He had a fresh face with a scattering of freckles across his nose and cheeks. He put a couple of coins on the counter and Elise shoved them back. I took a step forward as she slid a bear claw from the tray; it was covered with vanilla frosting, some of it seeping between the claws.

Elise held it out to him. He hesitated but finally reached out and took it. "I'm bringing it right back if it isn't better than the last one," he said, mimicking the woman exactly.

They both grinned.

"It's your own baking, after all," she said as he ducked outside.

She turned to the next person, and the bell over the door sounded again. A couple of teenagers came in, laughing and pushing each other. Would I ever have the chance to talk to her?

The ghost made a sound.

I moved closer to the counter and stood next to a man she was helping.

He pointed to a tray of rolls. "A dozen."

Elise shook a bag open and counted out the rolls. "Baker's dozen," she said. "Thirteen."

The man put the money on the counter, and a woman leaned over me. "I'm here for the cake," she told Elise.

The radio news interrupted the singer. *"The destroyer USS* Little *has been sunk by a kamikaze attack. Two hundred eighty survivors have been picked up by another ship."*

Not Rob's ship. My hand trembled and I reached out to steady myself. I hit the edge of the tray that held the frosted cake. Somehow it teetered on the edge of the counter.

Was it the ghost who tried to right it? Maybe I'd seen her small hand.

It was too late. The cake slid down the front of the counter, leaving smears of frosting on the glass and on my dress.

Elise was around in front in a moment. She didn't look at me or the cake, which was in a lump on the floor.

"An accident," she said to the woman. "I'll have another one in a few hours. I'll bring it to your house. It's on the corner of Eighth, right?"

I darted a look at the front door, but the old man was coming in with the dog. I turned and ran through the velvet curtain at the back of the store and went out the door.

"A cake," the voice was saying. "Only a cake."

I was in a yard with a falling-down wooden fence that surrounded a tangle of weeds. I didn't stop. I went through the gate along a gravel path, with fences on both sides of me, and headed toward the street. I held the little stone girl for comfort.

Where could I go? I didn't care.

But the ghost's voice in back of me said, "You've come a long way. Don't give up."

But I had.

Chapter 11

I was alone, almost alone. The ghost's tapping foot-steps were behind me. At the end of the alley was a street. The man, with his dog, Ella, walked by slowly, leaning on a cane.

A couple of boys were playing stickball, calling back and forth to each other. The man stopped to watch, Ella growling at them from behind his leg. The boys weren't worried; one bent down and patted her head.

Another smacked at the ball and missed. It bounced down the alley toward me, and the boy bounced after it.

"Get it!" he yelled.

I reached out, too late. The ball kept going, bounc-ing off the fence.

The boy grinned at me as he passed. I saw he was the one from the bakery. What had Elise called him? Andrew?

I stepped back and leaned against the fence as he scooped up the ball. "You'll never be a catcher for the Giants," he said.

"I'm a Yankees fan anyway," I called after him.

"Impossible," he said.

Then the man was gone, and the boys disappeared, one by one.

What was I going to do now?

How many things I'd broken at my foster mother's house! And there was Celine's almost-genuine Ming vase. But ruining the cake seemed so much worse.

A clock chimed somewhere nearby. Five in the afternoon. The day was endless.

Where could I go?

How could I take that long bus ride back to North River and walk up the hill to Celine's house?

I couldn't think of that.

Suppose I went back to the beach instead, to the silky sand and the waves that somehow led to Rob?

It would be dark soon, everyone gone from the beach. I'd be alone.

I *was* alone.

I stood there against the splintery fence, my feet pulsing with fatigue, my face sunburned from the beach.

"Go back," the voice said again.

I shook my head.

"At least to her garden, Jayna," the voice said. "The fence is high. You can hide and no one will see you there. You'll be safe."

I couldn't think of anything else.

We walked back to Elise's fence; it was as messy as the garden with jagged edges. There were spaces where some of the narrow slats must have been, like missing teeth on a Halloween pumpkin.

I pushed the gate open, then waded through the weeds. Some of them were stiff and brown from last year, but underneath was the green of new growth.

I sank down in the center of the garden, listening to the buzz, the click, the saw of contented insects. Near me, a cricket climbed a green spike of grass, bending it over. Above my head a house wren sang. A loud song for such a small brown bird.

Why did this garden remind me of the pond? There was no water, just a bit of mud that meandered around the side of the fence.

Still, there was something: the smell of things growing or the earth underneath.

I opened Theresa's case. "Catch a bug for yourself."

She lumbered out and stopped. How cautious she was. She raised one foot, her claws thick. She took one step, raised her foot high, and took another, the weeds flattening out behind her.

I pulled up a narrow blade of onion grass and sucked

on it, the edges sharp against my tongue. It tasted almost like a soup I sometimes made.

I took out Rob's stone and ran it over my forehead. It was cool against my face. I turned it over in my hands. For the first time, I realized the dark lines were ridges. I wondered what had made them, maybe hundreds of years ago. If only I were home in that house with the blue roof. If only Rob were safe.

All was quiet now. It seemed as if everything had gone still. Even the insects had stopped their chirping.

I sank deeper into the weeds. The sun was going down. I had a quick thought of winter, which was months away. But it would come, and when it did, where would I be?

I pictured the war in the Pacific, the island of Okinawa. Would it be over by then? Would Rob be home, telling me it had all been a mistake, that he'd never been missing? Would he say, *We'll open a restaurant in Brooklyn*? Would he say, *You'll make soup*?

The ghost sighed.

Theresa left a trail behind her as she moved slowly away from me. I closed my eyes, telling myself it was just for a moment. . . .

And slept.

When I awoke, it was almost dark. A square of light came from the kitchen window of the bakery. I saw Elise moving back and forth.

My grandmother?

I wanted that. I wanted that thin woman with the lilt in her voice to belong to Rob and me. Next to Rob's coming home, I wanted it more than anything.

Without thinking, I stood up. I was filthy, dirt on my legs, my shoes scuffed, and my dress! Wrinkled and stained. How could I . . .

"You could," the voice whispered.

I had to.

An old path led to the back door. She stood at the stove. Was she cooking something for her dinner?

I'd tell her that I'd stop and think from now on. I'd be careful. I'd never ruin a cake again . . . never.

I knocked on the door and she turned toward me, tilting her head.

"Please," I said, not sure that she could even hear me through the glass. But she came to the door and opened it. She was surprised to see me again, or maybe at the way I looked.

"Could I come in?" I asked. "Could I talk to you for a minute?"

Chapter 12

Elise nodded and stood back. There were chairs around a large floury table, and I sank into one, rubbing my eyes against the light.

"Are you hungry?" She glanced back at the stove. "I made potato pancakes with a little meat on the side."

I nodded, suddenly starving.

"There's something comforting about potatoes," she said. "Something soothing."

Last winter I'd cooked potato soup. And that was exactly what I'd called it: Soothing Soup.

The pancake she put in front of me was golden; the meat was spicy. I breathed in the steam that rose from it. I took huge bites. Celine would have had a fit. I tried to slow down.

Elise sat across from me, eating, too. I could tell she was watching me, but I didn't look up.

"I don't know what the meat is," she said. "I take whatever the butcher has these days."

"It's good," I whispered.

We kept eating, the sound of the wall clock clicking. I could see the ghost—part of her, anyway: a small hand with a ring on her finger.

"Where do you belong?" Elise said at last.

I didn't dare say *here*. But I wanted to say that I belonged in her warm kitchen, staying with her while I waited for Rob.

Instead, I told her that I broke things. I didn't mention Celine's vase, though. I raised my shoulders in the air. "I'm so sorry about the cake."

I began to cry silently. The tears slid down my cheeks and dripped onto my hands at the edge of the table, leaving dark spots in the floury wood.

"Save your tears for something more important than a cake," she said, smiling just a little.

"But the eggs, the butter . . ."

"This isn't the first time I managed without enough eggs or butter," she said, but still she looked a little worried.

I could see that. How could you run a bakery without eggs or butter?

"I was in another war," she said, "in France, when I was young. We called it the Great War."

I nodded. Mrs. Murtha had told us about that war.

I told her about Rob. "There are just the two of us," I said. "And now he's missing in action." It was hard to swallow. "His ship might have been hit by a kamikaze plane. I don't know."

Her face was sad. "Young pilots diving into ships. Some of them only seventeen years old. Such a waste of life. But you can't be alone. There must be an adult to take care of you."

I pictured Celine with the hairpiece over her eyes.

Then I remembered Theresa, outside somewhere in those high weeds.

I pushed back my chair. "I have a turtle." I darted toward the door. "Please, I just have to find her."

I waded in the sea of grass and weeds, then crawled through the old winding path where the growth wasn't as high, back and forth, calling softly, as if she could hear me.

I searched for her until it was too dark to see, then circled the fence with its huge spaces on the bottom. Those spaces were more than large enough for Theresa to have wandered through.

She was gone.

I went back to the kitchen door, which Elise had left open. She was setting out dough to rise, with the radio blaring war news: rings of destroyers around the island of Okinawa, many damaged, some sunk, but still many more alert, ready to fight.

The *Muldoon*.

Not ready to fight.

Gone under the water.

Elise turned to me, a dusting of flour on her face, wisps of hair escaping from her bun. "You're back?" She shook her head a little. "It's late. What are you doing here, child?"

"Please let me stay," I burst out.

I could see the shock in those turquoise eyes. "But where do you live?"

"Tell her," the voice said. "Say it."

"I lost my turtle. A beautiful turtle Rob and I call Theresa. Please let me stay. I'll find her in the morning. And then . . ."

"And then you'll go home." Elise spread out her thin hands. "You have to go home. You belong somewhere. I know that."

I didn't answer. How could I?

"I don't even know your name," she said.

I hesitated. Suppose I told her about Gingersnap?

"It's Jayna," I said.

Chapter 13

Elise looked out at the darkness. "You'll be safe here tonight. We'll sort it out in the morning. If I had a phone . . ." Her voice trailed off.

Tonight. It was a beginning. I was too tired to think of more.

She went ahead of me through the bakery, flipping off the light switch and opening a door to a narrow hall. Ahead of us was a long, curved stairway, with a shiny wooden banister that was smooth against my hand. I loved the feel of it.

What would it be like to live here? Really live here? To go up these stairs every night?

I felt a rush of air as the ghost went past me. Her

footprints appeared and disappeared, pressing down the carpet as she skittered up the stairs. "To belong," she whispered.

Yes, to belong.

My fingers felt a difference in the wood of the banister. Someone had gouged out . . .

Initials?

I traced them with my finger, hesitating on the step. *ML.*

Marie Louise?

My mother's initials?

Could that be?

On the next level, we passed a living room, and beyond that a dining room with a dark table as shiny as the banister. It was old, with scratches on the legs and a few on top.

I counted four doors on the top floor. Elise opened the first one, just off the stairs. It was a perfect room for me, tiny, with a bed and a dresser and faded red flowers in the wallpaper. It overlooked the street, the darkened windows of the dress shop and the bookstore across the way.

"You can shower," Elise said. "The bathroom is down the hall. And root around in the dresser for something clean to wear."

She ran her hand over the bedspread, smoothing out a wrinkle. "We'll call home in the morning. There's a phone in the stationery store around the corner. After that, you'll go back."

I opened my mouth, but what could I say? No one was there in our blue house. No one at all. And that was home.

"It's late," Elise said. "We'll talk about everything in the morning."

She smiled again and brushed my shoulder with her hand as she passed me and went out the door.

Tomorrow, I thought.

"Tomorrow," the voice echoed.

I was tired now, so tired that I slipped out of my blouse and skirt and left them bunched up on the floor. I went into the bathroom and stood in the shower with my head against the smooth tile wall, the water warm, my eyes closed.

I let the mud, and the grit, and the sand wash down the drain. And my tears, too. Tears for Rob, for Theresa. Who knew where they were?

I began to think about Elise and why I'd had that book. I remembered the day Rob brought me to the house with the blue roof. I'd wandered around from one room to the next, opening drawers, touching curtains. "Just tell me something else about our mother and father," I'd said.

"They were kind."

"Not that. Something different."

He raised his hands to his head. "Mom had ginger hair like yours. Her name was Marie Louise."

I knew all that. I wanted more. "What else?"

But that was it for that day. Rob was a quiet guy.

In the bedroom now, I found pajamas with tatted lace around the collar and a little more around the cuffs. I fell across the bed, my head on the pillow with its faint smell of lavender.

I went back to my skirt, reached into the pocket, and found the stone girl. I put it on the dresser opposite the bed, where I could see it in the dim light coming from the window.

I slid under the covers, so tired, so glad to be there, if only for one night.

"Sleep." Was that what the ghost said?

"Yes," I mumbled.

And then I was dreaming.

Chapter 14

Daylight edged around the brownstone houses across the way, turning the steps rosy colors. A tiny glass clock on the dresser said four-fifty-five.

A few minutes later, a church bell nearby chimed five times. From the window, I could see the steep roof and the cross on top of a church, blocks away.

I pulled the sheet over my head, telling myself to sleep. Eyes closed, I pictured ships sinking and planes spiraling into the ocean.

Hadn't Celine told me about a pilot and his crew that were stranded on a raft for a few weeks? They'd been saved when a seagull landed on the pilot's hat, giving them just enough food to get them through until they were rescued. But how often could that happen? A seagull!

The pilot had kept thinking of chocolate malteds. I'd heard that somewhere. Was that what Rob was thinking of? Malteds and ice cream?

"Soup," whispered the voice. "He'd think of your soup. And when he comes home, you'll make it for him."

"Asparagus soup," I said.

"Horrible."

I veered off. "Beef, then, thick with tomatoes and noodles, lots of noodles."

"Better." Was she smiling?

If only that would happen.

I was wide awake. Cooking tins rattled in the bakery kitchen below. Bread was baking, or rolls, and I smelled fruit and cinnamon simmering.

I remembered: Theresa! I had to find her.

In one of the drawers, I found a plaid dress with bone buttons that fit. I went downstairs to the kitchen. Elise stood at the table, rolling out dough. She glanced at me and nodded.

The boy from yesterday stood opposite her. His dark hair hung over his eyes. I hadn't combed my hair this morning; I didn't even have a comb.

I stared at Elise, the soft loop of hair against her neck, earrings like drops of snow, and an apron that covered her completely, rustling as she moved, so starched it could have stood by itself.

She worked quickly, twisting bits of soft dough into small braids, then put each one onto a metal tray in front of her.

As fast as she finished one of the rolls, the boy dipped a brush into a pan of melted butter. . . .

Not butter, but oleo, white margarine.

Elise nodded at me. "Doesn't taste exactly like butter," she said, "but we make do."

He coated each roll, almost as if he were splashing paint on a wall. He never stopped talking, even though I was sure he'd seen me standing in the doorway.

"No letters from my father," he said, facing Elise. "Fifteen days now. But that's all right. The war in Germany is over."

He turned to me. "He was in all the big battles. He's tough even though he doesn't look it. I saw him lift a stove once. I knew nothing was going to happen to him."

He talked so fast, it was almost as if he were a kite and I was trying to hang on, sailing along behind him.

Elise kept making gentle sounds as she worked with the dough.

I saw the cat carrier under the table. It wasn't empty! Theresa was back inside, looking like her usual calm self, blinking once, then closing her eyes.

I bent over to poke my fingers into the mesh; I ran my fingers over the edge of her shell. "Oh, Theresa." I looked toward the boy. "Did you find her? Where was she?"

"That carrier is a terrible place for a turtle," he said. He sounded like a commercial on the radio, one that said some soaps were so terrible they made holes in the wash.

"I know it isn't a good place for her, but for now . . ." Elise nodded a little.

"A box turtle." His voice rushed along. "People used to carve their initials into their shells, sometimes the dates. One lived about a hundred thirty-eight years. But you'll probably kill this one before she's ten, keeping her in a cage. . . ."

I opened my mouth to answer him angrily, but then I saw he was trying not to smile.

"Probably," I said. There was something about that face, that turned-up nose, his two chipped teeth, that made me want to smile.

Would we be friends?

But Elise said, "Jayna's going home today."

"With the turtle?" the boy asked.

"Of course with the turtle."

"She's mine," I said.

"Actually, she should be mine now," he said. "I found her. I read about that. Possession is nine-tenths of the law."

"Just try to take her."

"Tough girl." He nodded at Elise as she slid the tray of rolls into the oven.

"I can't go home," I said.

The bedroom upstairs with the red roses on the wallpaper, the church bells ringing, this enormous kitchen.

Elise, who might be my grandmother!

Elise wiped her hands on her apron. "Your family must be worried."

"You'd be worried if you were my grandmother?"

"Yes."

"I really can't go home," I said, almost bursting with it. "There's no one there. My brother, Rob, is somewhere in the Pacific, missing. There's only a landlady."

The boy looked sorry for me. "No family?"

Outside I heard a piercing whistle.

Elise and Andrew glanced at each other. Andrew was grinning now. "That's my sister, Millie. Time for school." He turned to me. "Don't kill that poor turtle while I'm gone," he said, and he was out the door.

Elise bent down to the stove, and I began again. "Celine, the landlady, really doesn't want me there. She wants her life back. I heard her say it, but I knew it anyway."

"Tell me about this landlady. Tell me about your brother."

And so I told her everything. I talked about Mrs. Alman at the last foster home, about Rob rescuing me.

79

I told her about Celine with the hairpiece; Celine, who was teaching me manners; Celine, whose vase was in a hundred pieces.

I talked until I was out of breath, and Elise got up from the table and poured me a glass of cool water from the faucet.

The only things I left out were what Rob had said about a grandmother, the recipe book, and the name Gingersnap. Instead I begged her, "Let me stay."

She sat there, head tilted, wisps of hair escaping from that bun. "So many children are displaced because of the war. Every war."

Displaced. Yes.

I wanted to tell her about what Rob had said, about finding the book, about the girl with braids, but Elise came to the table and sat opposite me. She reached out and touched my hands. "We lived in an old stone house until the Great War came."

Her head was bowed. I could see the part running through her hair. It was almost as if she were talking to herself, whispering, as if she'd forgotten I was there. "We couldn't stop to take anything with us but warm coats and our identity papers."

She shook herself and looked at me. "I know what we'll do." I could see it in her eyes. She was going to let me stay. But the bell jingled in front of the shop. The curtain was open, so I could see all the way to the door. It was the man with the little white pug.

Elise stood up. "It's Mr. Ohland and Ella, my two best customers. They want their breakfast."

She went through to the front and turned back. "We'll call that landlady together. We'll see what she says. Give me a minute and I'll go with you."

I looked up to see the ghost's fingers with my nail polish. Two of them were crossed.

Chapter 15

Elise led the way across the street.

"Could I use the phone?" I asked the man behind the counter.

"If you have a nickel." He grinned at Elise. He was an old man with crinkly gray hair and a mustache that moved up and down when he spoke. "On the side wall," he said.

Elise reached into her pocket, but I shook my head. "I have it."

I picked up the receiver. My hands were damp. Suppose Celine said no? Suppose she wanted me back right away?

"Number, please," the operator said.

The old man stacked bundles of newspapers against the other wall, talking to Elise as I waited for the operator to find Celine in North River.

I heard Celine's voice, almost as if she were standing next to me. "Wait, I have to sit down. I've been frantic. Jayna? Is that you? How could you run away like that?"

"I'm all right." I looked over my shoulder. Elise was still talking to the man. "I'm fine, really fine." I lowered my voice. "I'm with my grandmother."

"A grandmother?" Her voice rose in surprise. "How can that be? Why didn't I ever hear . . ." She was silent for a moment. "I'm glad you have someone."

It was my turn to be silent. I'd forgotten she could be that kind. But hadn't she reached out to me after I'd read the telegram? "I'm in Brooklyn."

"Brooklyn? How did you possibly—"

"A bus," I cut in. "Then I took the subway."

"Exactly where in Brooklyn?"

I ran the phone cord through my fingers. There was no help for it; I had to tell her. She'd be the one to get the news about Rob or his letters if they came. "She has a bakery. It's on Carey Street."

Elise was next to me now, her hand out.

"Listen, Celine," I said, "I'll let you talk to her."

I stood there, eyes closed. Please don't let Celine mention *grandmother*.

"Jayna's here," Elise said. "I'm not sure how you feel about her staying."

I stepped closer, trying to hear what she'd say. Whatever it was seemed fine.

"I'll take care of her," Elise said. "You can be sure of that."

Celine said something else.

"For a few weeks?" Elise said. "Yes, that's what we'll do." She handed the phone back to me.

"I don't know about all this." Celine sounded uneasy, worried. "Your brother's sent money."

"It's fine," I said. "He'd want you to have it."

"Will you call me?"

"Yes, all the time," I promised. I gave her the number of the stationery store phone. "If you hear from Rob, call. Call right way."

"Of course I will. But the money . . ."

"It's yours, Celine. Rob wanted you to have it."

She hesitated. "We'll talk about it when he's home."

When he's home.

I put the receiver down gently.

What did I care about money?

I cared about Rob. I cared about that bedroom with the roses. I cared about that kitchen, the pots hanging on one wall. Already I cared about Elise.

I pulled my hair back with one hand, my unruly ginger hair, curly hair. I'd wet it down, tie it back.

Mrs. Murtha's voice: *"You're as organized as your hair."*

I would be organized. I'd make Elise love me. I'd help. I'd take care of Theresa. I'd . . .

". . . do anything," the voice said. "I believe in you."

When Rob came back, we'd rent that empty shop next to the bookstore. We'd stay here forever, a family, back and forth across the street to the bakery.

As we left, Elise looked as uneasy as Celine had sounded. "We'll just have to see."

"Goodbye," the man called after us.

Back at the bakery, sun gleamed through the window.

Elise went to the front. I had time to see the kitchen. Rob would have loved it. I turned around slowly, looking at every corner. It was as if someone had dusted not only the table, but also all of it, floor, ceiling, walls. Flour floated in the air. It covered the window, the nests of pans stacked on a red countertop, and the old pots that hung on hooks over the table.

It was a perfect room, in a perfect place, except for the radio on a shelf. It wasn't loud, but it was clear: the announcer spoke about Okinawa, ground forces closing in on the Suri Temple area, which seemed to divide the island in half.

I stood entirely still. Then I turned off the radio.

"Good girl," said the voice. I turned. She was as dusty as the rest of the kitchen, her hair covered with it.

A floury ghost.

I crossed the room to the window, my shoes leaving imprints on the floor. The window was so coated with flour it was hard to see out.

85

I found a cloth and searched through the icebox for vinegar. I mixed the vinegar with water and found old newspapers. I knew how to wash a window, thanks to Celine.

Moments later, I stared through the glass, still dusty on the outside. If only I could tell Rob about everything. If only I could see him for even five minutes.

I went upstairs and reached for the stone girl. I held it in my hands, rolling it gently, thinking about that day at the pond, Theresa on a log, Rob and I both muddy. All of us gone now.

"Don't give up," I whispered to him.

I found Theresa's food. The box was nearly empty. Downstairs, I sprinkled it in the cage, watching as she snapped at the dark specks. I gave her water, then brought her to the garden and opened the cage door. I kept my eyes on her as she circled a gnarled little tree and then folded herself into her shell and slept.

I began to wash the outside of the window, thinking of the word *hope*, a breath of a word. I even said it aloud. If only Rob could hear me.

Please let him be alive.

Just get him home.

Just get him to Brooklyn.

Reaching into my pocket, I touched the stone girl again. It'd been around forever, tumbling off a mountain, rising up from the sea.

The outside of the window was harder to clean than the inside. Mud must have spattered up from a rainstorm, but after a few minutes, I could see the shine of the glass. Before I took Theresa back inside, I stopped to look at that overgrown yard.

It must have been lovely once. Along the jagged fence, small flowers were beginning to bud. Shiny leaves covered the tree.

I saw Elise come into the kitchen. She smiled at me through the window, then reached into the stove to pull out the tray of twisted rolls.

I went inside. "Let me cook something," I said. "Let me make soup for dinner."

"What would you cook?" Elise asked.

"Stew? A chicken stew with carrots? With noodles?"

"Really?"

"I can."

"You'll have to go to the butcher. See what he'll give you. Tell him you belong to . . ." She hesitated. "To the bakery. He'll put it on our bill." She hesitated. "And take the ration book from the shelf. You'll need the stamps for the meat." She pushed back her hair. "So much is rationed now. Sugar, coffee, meat. The list goes on and on."

I set out with her directions in my head. Two blocks left, one right, past the school . . .

The school.

I stood in front of that big red building. GIRLS it said over one door, BOYS over the other. The schoolyard was filled with kids.

I walked away quickly. I wouldn't pass that block again. Better that no one knew I wasn't in school for the rest of the term. How many days left? Only a few. Next fall, I'd go back.

The ghost came along behind me.

"Do you think a ship will find Rob? Do you think he'll really come home?" I asked slowly.

I was almost afraid to hear the answer.

"I'm not sure," she said, just as slowly. "We just have to believe it."

I sent him a message in my head. *I believe it.*

I found the butcher shop, HARRY'S MEATS written in flaking gold across the window, a banner with two blue stars: two men who were soldiers or sailors. Harry's sons? His brothers?

Inside, the butcher leaned forward. He wore a white cap on his head. "You look like someone I know."

I didn't ask who it was. I pretended it was Elise and just smiled. I held out Elise's ration book and my own money.

"Do you think I could have a chicken?" I asked.

"Why not? Anything for a girl with hair like yours."

He brought out the chicken and wrapped it. I handed him the money and tore a stamp out of the book.

"You look like that movie star with red hair, Maureen something."

A movie star.

I danced back to the bakery with the chicken in a brown bag under my arm.

Elise was waiting. "We forgot about school. How could we . . ."

"In September. Don't worry. I'm a good student. I'll make it all up then—you'll see." I crossed my fingers. "Top of the class."

She shook her head. "No, that won't work. If you're going to stay, you have to learn."

I put the chicken on the table. "Please, it's so near the end of the term. A new teacher, new kids! I can't."

"I remember that," she said. "I went to a new school and I couldn't speak English." She took a breath. "Still . . ."

I took the chicken to the sink and washed it. "Please," I said again.

"We could do this. Mr. Ohland was a teacher long ago. I wonder if he might be willing to sit with you."

Mr. Ohland with his kind face and his small dog, Ella.

Why not?

"Yes." I shook the drops of water off the chicken.

XXX

Hope Soup

INGREDIENTS

Chicken

Water

Oleo (too bad)

Salt, pepper, thyme

An onion or two

Noodles

(Easy, right?)

WHAT TO DO

Simmer the onions in the oleo.

Cook the chicken in the water.

Add everything else in with the chicken.

Take the chicken out and cut the poor old thing into pieces. (Careful, it'll be hot.)

Put the pieces back in the water.

Add the noodles.

Cook until it smells wonderful.

Keep breathing in.

Keep whispering "Hope," "Believe," "Soon," "Really."

XXXXXXXXXXXXXXXXXXXXXXXXXXXXXXXXXXXXXXXXXXXXXXXXXX

Chapter 16

I added a bay leaf I'd found in a jar on the pantry shelf and threw in another sprinkle of thyme. I tasted the soup as it cooked, blowing on the wooden spoon to cool it. I could feel that warm salty liquid going down, soothing me.

Hope.

I tried to keep thinking about that, even as I wondered what it was like to be far away from this warm kitchen, in a war, on a ship exploding somewhere in that huge sea.

Elise went back and forth between the kitchen and the bakery counter. I noticed that the bell over the front door hadn't rung in a long time.

She began to make coffee rings. "So little sugar," she said, scraping the bottom of the canister. When she was finished, they looked almost like Christmas wreaths, bristling with raisins and cherries.

She brought them out front, but still there weren't any customers, except for Mr. Ohland. He sat peacefully at a wrought iron table with Ella, waiting to begin my lessons.

I stirred the soup, then poured it into a large bowl to cool as Elise came back into the kitchen. She sat at the table with papers and a pencil, making rows of figures, erasing, beginning again.

I went outside, feeling shy, and slid onto a chair across from Mr. Ohland. Ella looked up at me, then retreated to the other side of the table, as far away from me as she could get on her leash.

"So," Mr. Ohland said. He asked me about the books I'd used in my school in North River, and I told him about learning the state's products.

He shook his head. "There's a war going on—it's just finished in Europe and raging now in the Pacific—and instead you're learning about the products of New York State."

"Gloves from Gloversville, lumber from Deposit." I smiled at him, reaching out with one foot to rub it gently against Ella's back.

Mr. Ohland ran his hand through his hair. "So what

started this terrible war? It's so complicated, so hard to unravel, but we're getting toward the end of it now."

How much I wanted to hear that.

He reached into his pocket and pulled out a small book of maps. "Picture islands scattered in the Pacific Ocean." He traced them with his wide fingers. "Some of them are the Japanese homeland; some of them farther out—"

"Like Okinawa," I said.

"Right."

"My brother's ship sank off Okinawa." I could hardly get the words out. "He's missing in action."

Mr. Ohland covered my hand with his, and even Ella seemed to move closer. He began again. "The greatest fleet ever amassed is there at Okinawa. Destroyers steam in rings around the island. American ships move closer. Our soldiers invaded the southern part of Okinawa, fighting their way forward."

I nodded.

"We'll read about war, and what happens to people caught in a war on both sides."

Elise came outside. "Lunch," she said. "Jayna's soup is ready. Would you like to try some?"

"Thank you, but it's time for Ella's walk."

In the kitchen, I rummaged through the cabinets and found thick beige bowls. I filled one for Elise and one for me, cut two slices of bread, then sat across

93

from her, not speaking, as she added and subtracted numbers.

She reached for a spoon absently, took some of the soup, and smiled. "Well. This is a surprise." She closed her eyes, leaning over the bowl, breathing in the steam.

She dipped her bread into the soup and brought it dripping to her mouth. "It's really wonderful."

Celine would have been horrified at that dipping and dripping. It made me grin.

"You have a gift," she said.

Rob had said, "No one makes soup like you do."

I dunked my bread into the soup.

It really was good. Not only was it just salty enough, but the taste of thyme was like the Thanksgiving turkey Rob had made.

"Rob said we belong here," I said without thinking.

"In Brooklyn?"

"Yes . . ." I hesitated, taking a breath, feeling my heart beat, ready to tell her. "I think I belong in this bakery."

She shook her head. "Look around. There are so few customers. I can't always get what I need for baking. Nothing tastes quite the same. Not enough butter. Eggs are sparse, and sugar. This war has to end soon or the bakery . . ." She stopped, her lips tight.

I saw the shadow of the ghost in the doorway.

"I think you're my grandmother." I whispered the

94

words, watching her face, seeing the surprise, the shock as she shook her head slowly.

"No, Jayna."

I sat there, frozen. I couldn't say a word. I couldn't even think.

The back door flew open. Andrew stood there, pushing in a girl who was a little taller than he was. Her pale hair was thick and braided, her eyes almost green. "I've come to see the turtle killer. I'm Millie, Andrew's sister."

I had to like her after hearing only those few words. Who wouldn't like that feisty girl, skinny as a pretzel, a million freckles, laughing with her crooked teeth?

She leaned over the table, put her arms around Elise's neck, hugging her quickly, then bent over Theresa's cage, whistling at her so softly it was almost a breath.

"Sit down, eat," Elise said. "Jayna's made wonderful soup."

I filled bowls for both of them and cut more bread.

"We had lunch in school," Millie said. "But I'm still hungry."

I looked at the clock. Where had the day gone? We sat at the table, eating. It was almost like having a family, if only for those few minutes.

Millie, like Andrew, never stopped talking. "The soldiers are coming home from Europe by points. The more points they have, the faster they get to a ship.

And Dad has points because he's married. Points for both of us kids. And he's been there so long, there are points for that."

She looked across at Andrew, and they smiled at each other. "But I've come about Theresa," Millie said.

Andrew answered before I had a chance. "She's just in a cage for now."

I stared at him. He'd made his voice sound exactly like mine. How did he do that? He rolled his eyes at me across the table.

Millie's mouth was full of bread. "We're going to save Theresa, Andrew, me, and what's your name . . . Jayna." She looked across at Elise. "That is, if Elise will lend us her garden."

Before Elise could answer, the bell jangled, and she went to the front through the curtain.

"She'll say yes," Millie said. "She always does."

Not always, not when I needed to hear it.

I looked from one to the other. Soup dripped from Andrew's chin. Millie had a little chicken on her cheek. "This is the best soup," she said, "even from a turtle killer." She was smiling, though, nodding at me. "Here's what we'll do. We'll fix the fence up a bit with more wood. We'll make a spot for Theresa, maybe with chicken wire if we can ever find some. And there she'll be, right as rain."

"Fine and dandy," Andrew said in someone's voice, which made them both laugh.

They began to talk about the fence and skipping school tomorrow.

"Playing hooky?" I said, a little shocked.

She looked at me. "When was the last time you were in school?"

I gulped. "Well . . ."

But they were laughing.

Millie wiped her mouth. "We'll get wood. We'll steal it right from under Betty's nose."

"We can't do that," I said. "I'm not going to steal. I'd never—"

"Watch and see," Andrew said in a high, breathy voice.

"That's the way Betty sounds sometimes." Millie opened the back door, grabbing my wrist in her skinny hand. "Let's go, Jayna. We haven't got all day to waste."

Elise came around the curtain, handing out ginger-snaps. "These are good," she said. "Andrew helped make them."

She hesitated. "Would you wait outside, kids, for a minute? I just need to talk to Jayna."

Chapter 17

Elise put her hand on my shoulder. "I wish you were my granddaughter. I love your face. I love the way you try to help. I love your cooking. You're a wonderful girl."

No one had ever said that to me. Not the foster mothers, not Celine, not even Rob. I felt the syrup of it in my chest and reached out to her. How thin her bones were. I was taller than she was.

"You're not my granddaughter," Elise whispered, "but I wish you were."

The syrup was gone. I swallowed over the burning in my throat. I put my hand in my pocket and ran my fingers over that stone girl. I had to find that recipe book. I had to show her.

"Go now," she said. "I'm happy you've made friends."

Outside, it was hard to keep up with Millie and Andrew. They raced along the alleyway, turned at the end, and streaked up Carey Street. I was out of breath, still thinking, *a wonderful girl*, then, *not my granddaughter.*

We ran to a hardware store with SMITH'S painted on the window. Tools were propped up in the window, hammers and saws, and a rusty lawn mower was just outside the door. *Hardly used, good value* said the sign.

"Betty's behind the counter," Millie said. "Get ready."

"What are you two up to?" A woman turned toward me. "Three of you. I'm outnumbered."

"We're here to steal wood," Andrew said. Did he still sound like me?

I stepped back.

The woman rested her elbows on the counter. "It had to be something like that. You've brought the turtle killer with you."

I blinked.

"This is our mother," Andrew said, in exactly the deep voice of the Shadow on the Sunday afternoon radio.

My mouth opened.

"They didn't tell you?" The woman ran her hand

99

through her hair that must have been like Millie's once but was shot with gray now.

I shook my head.

"Feel sorry for me." She smiled. "I have these two gangsters to take care of." She waved her hand. "And my husband's hardware store to run while he's still overseas."

She looked around. "I don't know one thing about hardware. I know about gardening." She glanced toward the display window. "As soon as Frank is home, I'm out of this store and back into the soil."

While she talked, Andrew and Millie dragged pieces of wood out of a bin in back.

I wanted to tell her about Rob, but her eyes were so kind I knew I'd cry if I tried to get the words out. Besides, the noise of planks being dragged along was enormous. Millie was singing "Deep in the Heart of Texas" at the top of her lungs. Andrew was whistling something else.

"I can pay for the wood," I said.

"No, you can't. I'm trying to do everything right. I'm trying to be a good person. I've been doing that from the day Frank joined the army. I thought that it would count to get him home, to get them all home, back where they belong."

"Not displaced anymore," I said.

She nodded. "Exactly."

She leaned over the counter. "He has our good-luck

charm with him, a little ring. It's mine. He wears it on a chain around his neck."

"Do you think that made a difference?"

I saw a flash of tears in her eyes. "Maybe not. But if he believed it would bring him luck, I hoped it would make him strong."

I had a quick thought, and then it was gone.

Andrew was jumping up and down now, holding his thumb. "Splinters all over this wood. You'd think the owner would get rid of them."

"You would." Millie dragged a pile to the front of the store. "Put it on my bill," she told her mother. "I'll pay you when I'm forty."

"I don't believe it." Her mother winked at me.

Andrew pulled a wagon from the storeroom. We loaded on the wood; then we zigzagged back up Eighth Avenue. "We'll hammer these up all over the place," Andrew said. "The fence will be a marvel. People will come to see it all the way from the North Pole."

"Bringing their polar bears down here with them," Millie said.

"Hope they're on leashes," I said, grinning at them.

We turned onto Carey Street, dragging the wagon, and dumped the wood into the alley. The noise was spectacular. Elise came outside, her hands up to her cheeks.

"Early tomorrow," Andrew said. "We can only take one day off from school."

"Ah, no," Millie said. "It will have to be the day after. I'm in a play tomorrow."

Elise frowned a little. "The next day is a school holiday?"

"You might say that," Andrew told her.

They ran back down the alley, the wagon wheels grating. Elise went back into the bakery, and I kept thinking about Coney Island and my suitcase. I touched the stone in my pocket. "Bring me luck," I whispered, not really believing it. "Or make me strong. I have to find that recipe book."

Chapter 18

I spent part of the morning with Mr. Ohland, who read aloud from a small book he'd found in the library. It was about the Great War, Elise's war.

Afterward, I went to the stationery store to call Celine. She was back to her old self, talking about how much she had to do, veering off to ask if I was behaving, helping my grandmother, and trying to be a lady.

I said yes to everything, staring out at Carey Street.

When we hung up, I went back to the kitchen, where Elise was preparing a jelly roll.

"I'm going to wander a little," I said. "I'm going to see Brooklyn, if that's all right."

See Coney Island.

Look for the recipe book.

Elise took the tray to the stove. "Be careful. Don't get lost."

"Not displaced," I said, smiling at her. "Not yet, at least."

I took the subway, standing near the door, swaying with the movement of the train. What was it that Andrew's mother, Mrs. Smith, had said, leaning over the counter? Was it something I should know about? Something I should remember about a ring?

Whatever it was, was almost there, but it just wouldn't come to me.

My mind veered to the suitcase.

If only I could find it.

I got off at the Coney Island stop and walked the few blocks toward the boardwalk. On the beach, I picked up shells, running my fingers over them, then dropped them back gently onto the sand. A seagull swooped low over the water, wings outstretched, fishing.

I wandered around the curve of the sea. The waves were high and rough. Suppose Rob was on a raft? Something so small could easily turn over in an angry ocean. Oh, Rob.

I glanced over my shoulder at my footprints as they filled in with water. The waves left foam on the water's edge; the tide was coming in, and the sand was pulled back into the sea.

I kept glancing up toward the boardwalk, trying to remember where I'd been, where I might see the suitcase again. All the benches looked the same.

I bent down, cupping my hands for a scoop of salty water and raising it to my face. An old man sat on a beach chair in front of me, reading the paper, war news printed huge and black on the front page: *Yanks fighting fiercely in Okinawa.*

I realized there was space under the boardwalk, enough room for a person to stand or sit. Enough room for a suitcase? I looked back across the beach at brown striped umbrellas, a half-finished sand castle, turned over beach pails.

Two women with kerchiefs covering their hair talked to each other as they walked along. I passed them and the sand castle. I went up toward the boardwalk, to that shady space underneath, and circled around an empty jar of Noxzema and a few broken bottles. There was an old orange beach blanket, faded and torn, but the suitcase wasn't there. Of course it wasn't. I kept walking along, looking underneath, the sand shifting under my feet. I found stray papers, magazines, and toys, but nothing of mine was there.

I went back up on the boardwalk and kept walking, searching. Where had I sat that first day?

How long ago it seemed.

And then, wedged under a bench, almost like a miracle, was the book, pages open and blowing a little in the wind. I picked it up; it was thick with salt from the sea. Some of the ink had run. Whole pages were blurred; they'd disappeared in their own sea of blue ink.

The photograph was gone.

But at least I had the book. The suitcase didn't matter. Everything I needed right now was here, the book and the stone girl in my pocket.

That was what Betty had said. Now I remembered. Her husband had carried the ring with him; he'd believed it would bring him luck.

I sat there looking out at those rough waves; no swimmers today, just rolling green water rising up and up, then folding back over itself.

Rob needed luck.

And I had our luck in my pocket.

"It's our luck," I called out over those waves. "I have it for you."

He couldn't hear me; I knew that. But would he be thinking of me? Would he be determined to stay alive so we'd be a family together? I kept touching the book.

But suppose . . .

Suppose he had that stone girl?

On the subway, I looked around for a lock of hair, for a pink sock, for soft hands. But she was nowhere. "Where are you when I need you?" I asked.

She didn't answer.

I closed my mouth; a couple of kids were watching me, thinking I was talking to myself.

Maybe I was.

It was late in the afternoon now. The sun was just disappearing over the brownstone houses when I opened the back door to the bakery. My face was stiff from the salt air at the beach.

Elise sat in the kitchen, a pan of dough set to rise in the center of the table. She was looking at those papers of hers, bills, I supposed, working with a pencil and frowning.

I put the book in front of her on the table, the cover bent; the pages were sticky under my fingers. Her writing was there, though. She had to know it was hers.

She reached out and touched it gently, then my wrist.

"It's good luck," I said.

She opened her mouth to say something.

"Wait," I told her. "I'll make soup first."

"Yes, and then we'll talk."

I went to the stove, smiling.

This was why I'd come to Brooklyn.

XX

Good-Luck Soup

(You have to love potatoes.)

INGREDIENTS

Lots of potatoes, peeled and sliced
(See what I mean?)

A couple of leeks (No leeks? Chop up a little onion.)

Some good stock

A chunk of lard

WHAT TO DO

Melt the lard. Don't let it burn.
Don't let your fingers burn, either.

Add the leeks and simmer a little.

Add the stock and all those potatoes.

Cook for only about twenty minutes.
(It's lucky that it's all so fast.)

How about a little salt? A little pepper?

Done!

XXXXXXXXXXXXXXXXXXXXXXXXXXXXXXXXXXXXXXXXXXXXXXXXXXXX

Chapter 19

Elise put her papers away in the small cabinet against the wall. Without speaking, we set the table together as we waited for the soup to thicken.

How could she not believe I was her granddaughter now?

But when I began to speak, she tilted her head the way she always did, holding up her hand. "Wait," she said softly.

It wasn't until the bread was cut into chunks and the soup was in bowls on the table that she began at last.

"It was a terrible war," she said, "the Great War. We lived in a French village near Germany. Only a river separated us from the German border and the fighting."

She'd told me part of that before, but I listened to every word, my eyes on hers, hungry to hear, my spoon halfway to my mouth.

She closed her eyes for a moment. "In the early morning, when the sun was just coming up over the river, we heard the huge guns firing, coming closer. I remember my mother pulling off her apron. . . ."

My great-grandmother?

"She ran from the house to the stone barn, setting the cow free to wander, shooing the chickens away, while my father hitched our old horse to the cart. All the while they were shouting things to me: 'Your warm coat, put it on.' And to my brother . . ."

An uncle?

" 'Take the quilts from the beds. Bring them outside, spread them in the cart.' " She took a sip of the soup. "So good," she said, almost whispering. "Potato soup."

"Good-luck soup." I took a sip from my bowl. The soup was hot and thick.

I pictured Elise at my age, shrugging into her coat, the braids that circled her head coming loose, and her brother . . .

"What was his name?"

She looked startled. It was almost as if she'd forgotten I was there.

"His name was Michael. He was a year younger than I was. He clattered from the bedroom in back, dragging the quilt I'd stitched with my mother. In the kitchen, I turned one way and then another, not knowing what to do. My mother called, 'Take the eggs in a towel, the sausage in the larder.' My hands were trembling, and as I pulled the bowl of eggs toward me, I dropped them. They spattered on the stone floor, all dozen of them, the brown shells in pieces, shards from the bowl everywhere."

Just as I would have done, broken what was important. Elise nodded. To me? To herself? But I didn't think she was remembering that I dropped things and broke them as well.

She began again. "I stepped through the pieces of the bowl, the slimy eggs, and reached for the sausage. I saw the cookbook I'd labored over from the time I was able to write."

She reached out and touched the book that lay between us.

"The recipes I'd copied as my grandmother taught me how to work with yeast, how to roll dough," she went on. "I couldn't leave it. My dress had no pockets; neither did the coat I'd pulled over my shoulders. I wrapped the sausage in paper, tucked the paper parcel under my arm, and took the recipe book, too. All the time my mother was calling, 'Come. Come now, children.'

"The army had reached our side of the river. The guns boomed, almost at our village. But I remembered my doll, called Lena, after my aunt who lived in Colmar. She was a sweet doll with a porcelain face and a cloth body. She wore the clothes I'd sewed for her, a long dress with a holiday apron, and a hat with feathers I'd plucked from our hen."

I swallowed, putting my spoon down on the table, the soup cooling.

Elise was looking out the window that I'd washed, streaked again with flour. "How could I leave that doll?" she said. "I went back through the house, searching for her in the armoire, on the bed, and there she was on the windowsill, small and dainty, looking at me with her lovely glass eyes. I picked her up and ran, holding out the sausage package and the book to my brother in the cart.

"My father and mother were in front. 'Hurry, hurry,' they were calling, panic in their voices. I climbed up, ripping my coat, losing the doll's hat with the feathers.

"My brother, Michael, wasn't sad about leaving our house, our village, but for my parents and me, it was another story. My mother turned toward us; tears streaked her cheeks. I leaned against Michael. I looked at our house, at the bare plum trees that surrounded it, then at the narrow dirt lane in back of us.

"Another cart was lumbering behind us. My friend sat high up in front. There was a sudden loud noise, like a clap of thunder, the sound of a cannon. Michael was so startled that he dropped the parcel with the sausages, and I just managed to reach out for them."

Tears came down Elise's cheeks; she'd forgotten the soup. She spread out her hands, looking at me.

"But it was too late for the little book," she said. "It fluttered down off the cart, the pages riffling, onto the dirt road. And as we moved on, I watched the cart, just behind us. The wheels just missed the book."

Elise and I glanced down at the book. "How far it's come," she said.

"It has your name in it," I said. "And the address of the bakery."

She picked up the book and opened the pages, but the page with her name was torn. We could see the large *E* and *Carey Street*, but that was all.

"Ah. I see." She put her arms around me. "It's not my name, Jayna, but now I know who you are. Of course I do."

Chapter 20

The bell jangled in front, and jangled again. Elise shook her head. "There's so much more. Just wait, Jayna."

She wasn't my grandmother. I felt those words in my head. Elise didn't belong to me. Neither did this bakery. And I loved them both.

I was alone.

Elise ran her hands across my shoulders, then touched my cheek before she went through the curtain into the bakery.

I turned, hoping to see the ghost, hoping to hear her whisper something, telling me what that meant: *I know who you are.*

But everything was still. Motes of flour rose in the air, and the oven made its own sounds as bread baked. I went out the back door, leaving the spoons, the napkins, the bowls of half-congealed soup on the table.

I sprinkled the last of the dried insects over Theresa's cage, watching her snap at them, then stood breathing in the smell of the greenery growing in the garden.

What was that sweet smell?

I saw a patch of strawberries, the early fruit red and plump. I wiped the tears from my cheeks, then picked them and dropped them into my outstretched dress. I left them in the colander in the kitchen.

I could hear Elise in front talking to a customer. The bell jangled again. When we wanted the bakery to be busy, it never was. But now, when I wanted so much to hear what Elise had to say, more people were coming in.

I went upstairs, trailing my fingers along the banister to feel the *ML* letters. They might not have been my mother's initials; they could have been anything.

In my room, I sat on the edge of the bed, looking out the window. I had so much to think about, so much to wonder about.

What would Rob say to all of this?

Something was there in my mind again.

The hardware store.

Mrs. Smith: "He has the good-luck charm; he'll believe in it and it will make him strong."

Rob: Holding up the stone girl that day in the pond. "She might bring us luck."

The stone girl.

Why hadn't I given it to him the day he left?

But there was something I could do.

The ghost sat on top of the dresser, one bare foot resting on the thick drawer knob, a little pink polish on each of her toes. I saw her hand, just for a moment, her fingers raised, and I went toward her.

"Don't come too close, Jayna," she said. "I don't know why, but that's not allowed."

I held up my own hand. "All right. But I want you to do something for me. For Rob."

Did I see her nod?

I reached out and slid the stone next to her on the dresser doily. "I want you to take it to him."

"How can I do that?" she said. "I'm here to take care of you. How can I search the huge Pacific Ocean—" Her voice broke off. "And we don't even know . . ."

She began to disappear. Her foot faded; her hand was gone.

I hit the wall with my fist. The noise shocked me. Pain shot through my knuckles and up my arm. "Don't you dare leave me. You've followed me everywhere. What are you here for if not to help? I need you."

The foot moved a little; the fingers curled themselves together.

116

"He has to be alive," I told her. "He has to feel strong. He has to believe he'll come home."

She shook her head, the lock of hair swinging.

"I will stay here." My voice was fierce. "I will find out who I am. And you will go to him, to my brother, who is the most important person in the world to me. You will give him our good-luck stone girl."

I could almost see her crossing the country, reaching the West Coast, searching the Pacific Ocean for him. "You can go anywhere in the world," I said.

Was he alive?

I brushed away that thought. He had to be alive. He had to be on a raft somewhere.

"You will put it in the raft where he can see it. Whisper to him that he has to come home, that I'm waiting for him, that he has to hold on until someone finds him."

I stopped. It was enough.

She was silent. Then, "He has to come home," she echoed. "Jayna is waiting. He has to hold on until someone finds him."

"Yes. Exactly that."

"I'm not sure if I can. . . ."

"Be sure."

"I'll try," she said, and she was gone. The little stone girl was gone, too.

I'd just have to wait.

I went downstairs, back into the kitchen, and knelt by Theresa's cage. "We're going to fix a place for you, too."

Elise was still in the bakery. I turned on the radio as I washed and dried the bowls carefully and put them back in the cabinet. The Andrews Sisters were singing "Don't Sit Under the Apple Tree."

The radio crackled. The music was cut off.

"Okinawa has fallen," the radio announcer said. I could hear the excitement in his voice.

All those men on the island, both our side and the other side! All the displaced people! Were the destroyers moving away, and was Rob somewhere in that empty sea?

"A huge step toward the end of the war," the announcer said.

I picked up the blue recipe book and put it on a shelf, where it would be safe.

And then Elise called, "Jayna, let's talk."

Chapter 21

Elise came into the kitchen. "I've put the *Closed* sign on the door. Now it's really time for the two of us to talk. We'll go up to the living room."

On the stairs, she stopped and took my hand. "Feel the initials," she said. "Your mother's."

Tears began to slide down my cheeks. My mother.

We went into the living room with its dark shiny furniture. The late sun streamed in across the patterned rug as we sat together on the couch.

"I should have known the minute you walked into the bakery," she said. "That lovely hair, the cake sliding down the front of the counter. So much like your mother. Like your grandmother." She smiled. "Who else could you be but Marie Louise's daughter, Elise's granddaughter?" She shook her head. "Who else could cook the way you do?"

I wrapped my arms around myself. *Like my mother. Like my grandmother.* They were gone long ago. But still they were mine; they belonged to me.

She patted my hand. "The day we left our village, our cart lumbering down that dusty lane, we were looking back at the house and the little recipe book fluttering on the road. . . ."

I could see it, the cart, the lane, the neighbor's cart following.

"I stretched out my hands for that book," she said. "Of course, it was too late. But Elise, in the cart behind us, jumped off, catching the hem of her dress, the great wheels just missing her. She scooped up the book, reached out to hold on to the side of the cart, and was back up, waving it at me. I could see what she was saying, even though I couldn't hear her. 'It's safe,' she called. 'Safe, Madeline.'

"I called back, sending her a kiss, 'It's yours now. Keep it forever.'"

"Madeline?" I couldn't keep the shock from my voice. "You're not Elise?"

"Elise was my best friend," she said.

We were both quiet for a moment. Then she spread her hands. "Years later, the two of us came to Brooklyn. We decided to open a bakery. Why not? We both baked;

we both loved the yeast rising, rolling the dough, adding cinnamon and raisins. We loved making the pies, the cakes, the croissants, the Florentines, the gingersnaps. We went back and forth for a name for our bakery. Should it be Madeline's? Should it be Elise's?"

She was smiling now. "Elise won. Elise always won. By that time she had a husband, and a baby girl, so we named the bakery after that baby. Gingersnap."

My mother. Gingersnap, like me.

"Oh, that child, Marie Louise. She clattered up the stairs, carved her initials in the banister, climbed out the back windows, cooked even better than Elise and I could. She used that little recipe book, staining it with buttery fingers, with melted chocolate. She was our delight."

I was smiling. I could see her.

"She mixed up our names. I became Elise instead of Madeline, her mother something else, a made-up name for Mama."

Should I call her Elise or Madeline?

She knew what I was thinking. "Either one," she said. "Mr. Ohland calls me Madeline, but Andrew and Millie's parents call me Elise."

"Madeline?" I felt the word on my tongue. But I'd called her Elise from the beginning, so it had to be that.

Elise began again. "Our Marie Louise was married here, then lived in Brooklyn until she and her husband,

Claude, moved upstate because of his work. And then there was the accident.

"I was glad that your grandmother was not alive to know what had happened." She shook her head. "Such a heartache. And to think of you and Rob in foster homes. I didn't know that. If only I had." Her mouth was trembling. "So if you want to stay for a while, until your brother comes home . . ."

Staying here! I'd be in the bedroom with roses and the bakery kitchen. I could look out the window toward the subway, waiting for Rob. I threw my arms around her.

Soup came into my head. "Could I . . . ," I began, and started over. "Would you like to use some of my soup in the bakery?"

She didn't stop to think. "That's the best idea. I love your soup."

Later we locked up and went upstairs to bed. I heard the church bells chiming, counting with them as they tolled eleven times. I fell across the bed. So much had happened today, so much to tell Rob. "The ghost is coming," I whispered. "Just hold on."

XX

Waiting Soup

INGREDIENTS

A couple of cups of strawberries

Some orange juice

A cup of yogurt

Vanilla

A little sugar

WHAT TO DO

Simmer those strawberries on the stove
with the orange juice.

Stir and wait.

Cool.

Strain.

Add the yogurt, the vanilla,
and some sugar to the strawberries.

Put it all in the icebox.

Wait until it's really cold.

Spoon it into cups.

Eat it, at last.

XXXXXXXXXXXXXXXXXXXXXXXXXXXXXXXXXXXXXXXXXXXXXXXX

Chapter 22

It was going to be a hot day. The sun glinted off the kitchen window, turning the panes orange. I fed Theresa, then took her outside to rest in her cage under the tree that was filled with buds.

A plum tree?

Back in the kitchen, I half listened to Elise talking to Mr. Ohland at the table outside, words and half sentences: "Tokyo, Japan . . . War over this year?"

Early this morning there'd been no time for Elise and me to talk, no more than "Are you all right, Jayna?"

No more than a nod from me.

We'd both smiled and reached out to hug each other.

Now I heard the grinding sound of the wagon coming along the back alley. The door banged open and Millie and Andrew burst into the kitchen.

"Smells like something sweet in here," Millie said, twirling around the floury table.

"Like strawberries from the bushes outside," Andrew said in a Lone Ranger voice.

I nodded. "I made a cold soup with them. It has to chill. That's the hard part. You have to wait and wait, wait forever."

"Crazy," Andrew said.

Millie opened the top door of the icebox, leaning in. "Looks good. I hate to wait. Could I just stick my finger in for a quick taste?"

Her hands didn't look all that clean.

"Just kidding." She grinned and waved her fingers at me.

I hated to wait, too.

I pictured Rob walking up Carey Street, his duffel bag over his shoulder. He'd pass the dress shop, the bookstore, and I'd stand outside, waiting until he saw me, really saw me, before I'd run down the block, circling kids playing stickball, crossing the street, calling out, "I'm here, Rob! I'm here."

Andrew opened the back door again. "Let's get started."

I took a last look toward the front of the bakery,

through the open curtain. Elise and Mr. Ohland were outside, heads together at the table. I followed Millie and Andrew out the back door.

Andrew grinned at me as he leaned over Theresa's cage. "That Jayna is evil as Ma Barker," he told the turtle in an unfamiliar voice. "But we'll set you free soon."

He laughed, and I knew it was a voice I'd heard on the radio. Was it the Shadow?

Theresa stared up at him, unblinking, and I felt my mouth curve up, almost smiling.

Andrew looked up at the sky. "Summer's here." He looked at Millie. "And *General Hershey*, the troop ship Dad is coming in on, will dock in New York. It'll be soon, really soon. We just heard last night."

Millie grabbed my hands. "We're all going to meet him. My mother's been saving the last bit of gas in the car and we'll be there, waving when he comes in."

She leaned forward, still holding my hands hard. "I hardly remember what he looks like."

I squeezed her hands back.

Someday it will be Rob, hurrying up the subway steps.

Andrew grabbed a hammer and a box of nails from the wagon. He picked up one end of a board. "How about a little help here?"

I rushed over and helped him rest the board against an open space in the fence.

"It looks terrible," Millie said.

It really did. The board didn't fit; there were still spaces so you could see the alley beyond it.

"And we haven't even begun," Andrew said. "We have to add dozens of boards."

Elise and Mr. Ohland appeared at the back door. Mr. Ohland walked along the fence, running his hand over the splintery wood. He shook his head. "Not this way. It will never work."

"But it's the only way I can figure out," Andrew said.

"There's always another way," Mr. Ohland said in his schoolteacher voice.

I knew Andrew wanted to say, *Which way?* I could see he was bursting with it.

Millie said, "We have only today. We can't be playing hooky every two minutes."

Mr. Ohland frowned and looked at his watch. "I suggest the two of you get yourselves to school."

"We're a little late for that," Millie said.

"Never too late," Mr. Ohland said. "Hurry now."

They backed away, Andrew shrugging at me, Millie grinning, and left for school.

We went back into the kitchen, Elise, Mr. Ohland, and I, to sit at the table while Elise warmed yesterday's biscuits and made coffee.

Mr. Ohland reached for a pile of books on the counter. "I brought these for you this morning. History books, stories of our country."

They were already covered with a fine dusting of flour.

He grinned at me. "You can read while I think about that fence."

He took a sip from his cup. "Not quite the coffee it was before the war, but still, hot and good."

I poured coffee for myself and filled it to the top with milk, then began to turn the pages of the book.

Mr. Ohland swallowed his coffee. "The whole fence has to come down," he said. "We'll have to begin again. We can always do that."

Elise nodded. "Yes. We can do that."

Chapter 23

It was early the next morning. I was still in bed, finishing one of Mr. Ohland's books about people exploring the country, traveling down rivers, climbing mountains, fighting over the land.

I went to the open window, where a warm breeze was blowing in. I could see down Carey Street, the tall brownstone houses on each side, all the way to the subway. People hurried down the stairs, taking two at a time; a few were coming up after working a late shift somewhere. I pictured seeing Rob, his duffel bag over his shoulder, alive and safe.

A car horn blared. I opened the window to see a dark Ford coming up the street. Andrew and Millie leaned out the back window. "We're bringing our dad home!" they yelled.

"Elise," I called. "Hurry."

A moment later Elise stood next to me, our heads out, both of us waving.

As the car passed, I called out to them, "I'm so glad."

Before there was time for more, we heard a crash from the backyard as Mr. Ohland tore down the fence.

Downstairs I told Theresa, "Take a quick walk, but then it's back in the cage for now." I touched her lovely thick shell, ran my finger over her leathery tail. "Hang on, girl. Your garden will be ready before you know it."

I was happy for Theresa, happy for Millie and Andrew, who had a mother, a father, a sister, a brother.

If only . . .

Still munching the last of his honey bun, Mr. Ohland cut into my thoughts with the noise of the hammer. I watched him drive nails into the boards as he called over his shoulder, "All right, Jayna, where is Japan? What's our new president's name?"

We went back and forth between the sharp bang of the hammer. Where was the Japanese mainland? What was the capital?

I knew everything he asked, and he turned to grin at me. "Not bad, miss."

All day, we went from the bakery to the kitchen to the garden. Elise baked; I cooked soup. We brought iced tea and gingersnaps out to Mr. Ohland.

That night, Elise and I left the kitchen window wide open as we washed the dishes and slid them into the rack. The buzz and click of the insects was loud, and the smell of the new plants was sweet.

Dinner over, Elise took a walk while I went upstairs to read another of Mr. Ohland's books. I touched my mother's initials before I reached my room.

I stopped at my bedroom window, looking down Carey Street. An older man came up from the subway station and a few minutes later, a woman. She struggled with a small suitcase, stopping to rest. No wonder, she was wearing impossibly high heels. She looked one way and then another uncertainly before she came closer.

How familiar she looked.

I rushed out of my room and flew down the stairs to the kitchen. Already I could hear tapping on the glass door in front, first softly, then insistently.

"I'm coming," I called. "Coming right away."

She was always impatient. What was she doing here? It had to be bad news. Terrible news.

I went through the curtain into the bakery remembering. *Hiding in the bedroom closet, the feel of a silk dress between my fingers, the telegram waiting downstairs, Celine as she put her arms around me.*

I opened the door and, in spite of myself, held out my arms. "Celine!"

"Yes," she said, hugging me.

Whatever the terrible news might be, I was glad to see her, hairpiece askew, a dot of rouge high up on one cheek.

"News of Rob?"

She shook her head. "No."

I pulled her inside, took her suitcase, and sat her down in a chair at the table. Tomorrow's soup was in the refrigerator, a soup with bits of broccoli. I warmed it and cut her a thick chunk of bread. "Eat."

"It was a terrible trip," she said between spoonfuls. "The bus ride was endless, and the subway rattled along, so crowded I had no place to hang on."

"Yes, I remember."

I heard Elise coming back from her walk and called to her. "It's Celine, our landlady."

Elise came into the kitchen, smiling. "How lovely to see you."

"And you're the grandmother," Celine said.

Elise smiled. Amazing. She wasn't one bit bothered about Celine appearing without warning or being called the grandmother. She went to the stove, running her hand over my shoulder as she passed, and poured three cups of coffee. Then she sank into a chair between us, waiting, as I was, for Celine to finish her soup and tell us why she'd come.

At last, the soup and the bread were gone. "The reason I'm here . . . ," Celine began, and broke off to take a sip of her coffee. "It was my duty."

Under the table, I felt Elise's hand reach for mine.

"I know what it's like to be alone," Celine said. "And now that Jayna's brother is gone, I had to be sure . . ."

Gone.

I couldn't breathe.

Elise's hand was clutching mine so tightly I felt as if my bones were crunching together.

"Gone?" Elise said.

"Well, we haven't heard anything," Celine said, "so I had to be sure Jayna is happy here. If not, she can come back with me. Stay forever." She sounded breathless as she leaned forward to Elise. "She's a very nice girl, you know."

Oh, Celine.

She'd surprised me again.

At last we went upstairs. "We have a cozy room for you," Elise told her.

I fell into bed thinking of Celine's words: *I know what it's like to be alone.*

Chapter 24

Where was the ghost? Would she ever come back? Would she ever tell me what had happened to Rob?

In the morning, the fence was finished, the wood smooth and perfect.

That afternoon, Andrew's family arrived. We pulled up weeds and Mrs. Smith planted marigolds, daisies, and tomatoes, then herbs for my soups: basil, lemon parsley, dill, and oregano.

Mr. Smith came along carrying a huge bag of cement. He was bent over, so I could see a small bald patch in his brown hair.

"He's building a wall," Andrew said, just like the announcer on *Gang Busters*.

"No, it'll be steps that go from the kitchen to the fence," Millie guessed.

I knew, but Mr. Smith said it for me. "It'll be a small pool for the turtle. So let's dig." He raised his arms high. "Good to be home. Just smell those pies baking in the kitchen."

"Hey." Andrew pointed. Ella, the little pug, was standing in front of Theresa's cage, staring in, and Theresa had moved to the front, so their noses were almost touching.

"A staring contest," Andrew said.

"Ah, Ella's found a family." Millie wiped dirt off her face.

The bakery bell kept jangling. More people were coming to the bakery now. "Do you think they're getting used to oleo instead of butter and less sugar in the recipes?" I asked Elise.

"It isn't that." Elise shook her head. "It's the *We have the best soup* sign in the window. People are buying your soup every day."

⟨⟩

At the end of the week, just before the cement was dry, Mr. Smith lined us up at Theresa's pool to sink our handprints in around the edge: Elise's thin ones, Celine's plump ones, Mr. Ohland's, Mrs. Smith's with the imprint of her ring, and Andrew's, Millie's, and mine.

Last, Mr. Smith knelt down to dig in the year: 1945. "Someday soon," he said, "the war will be over, and the rest of the guys will come home from the Pacific."

I knew he wanted to give me hope.

Celine had been with us a week. Every day she talked about going home, but Elise said, "Stay a little while. See the garden finished."

Then Celine would sit back, pushing her hairpiece into place, reaching for one of Elise's Florentines or a crusty end of rye bread, listening to Mr. Ohland's lessons, interrupting. . . .

That Celine! But I couldn't be angry with her anymore. I heard Rob's voice in my head: *a good friend.*

Now the garden was finished.

"Shall I bring Theresa to the pond?" I asked.

"The poor thing hasn't had a real bath in weeks," Andrew said.

Elise held up her hand. "We'll have to have a grand celebration for that. Tables outside, candles, and a lovely dinner."

I went back inside and began to cut vegetables for a soup. I listened to everyone talking. It was cool in the kitchen, though. I could hear faint drips of water in the icebox.

I stood entirely still; something was different. A breath of air against my cheek? I turned slowly; faint fingerprints marked the floury table.

My hand went to my throat. "You're back."

Her fingers drew lines in the flour. "I tried," she said. "I'm not sure. I dropped the stone down on the lifeboat. Such a small stone. Such huge waves. It seemed as if the whole ocean were tilting in that typhoon. We have to hope. . . ."

There was that word again. *Hope.* But it wasn't enough. Not nearly enough. "Is he alive?"

"I don't know, Jayna."

All that, and nothing had changed. I sank into one of the chairs and put my head on the table, feeling the flour against my cheek.

"We must hope," she said. "That's all we have." Her fingers fluttered across my shoulder. "I have to leave you tonight."

"No, please," I said.

"I was here to help you find a family," she began. But the door opened. Mr. Smith and Andrew came in. I stood up quickly, wiping my face. I watched them wash the table and bring it outside.

By now it was almost dark and Elise was lighting tiny candles. I had to bring the soup outside. I couldn't disappoint everyone, no matter how terrible I felt about what the ghost had told me. "Don't go yet," I said over my shoulder.

Everyone was there as I set the soup tureen down in the center of the table.

"It's time for Theresa to try her pool," Andrew said.

I nodded and opened the door of her cage. She was cautious, but only for a moment. She left claw marks in the soft earth and headed straight for the pool, sliding down the sloped side and into the water.

We admired her swimming, head up. Ella stood at the side of the pool, watching her anxiously as we sat at the table.

"Right about now," the ghost whispered.

In the glow of the candlelight, I looked at all of us at the table. Andrew was pretending to lead a band in honor of Theresa, while Millie drummed on the table with her soup spoon.

Celine looked as if she'd faint at their manners. She caught my eye and shook her head, as if I'd agree.

Across from me, Mr. and Mrs. Smith leaned toward each other. When they saw me glance at them, they both smiled.

Mr. Ohland wasn't sitting yet. With one hand on Ella's collar, he studied Theresa in her new home.

Elise set a tray of bread on the table, then put her arms across my shoulders. "Do you see what you've done, Jayna? You've brought us together."

"No, it was Theresa," I said.

"Don't forget about me," the ghost whispered.

I felt something in my chest, a warmth that went up

to my throat. I wanted Rob to be here. I wanted that more than anything. But here was a family, my family. I knew I'd have them forever.

I heard the ghost for the last time. "Yes," she said. "At last."

XX

Family Soup

INGREDIENTS

A bunch of frankfurters from Harry, the butcher

A can of baked beans from Mrs. Smith's pantry

Chopped parsley from Theresa's garden

Some of that beef stock I made last week

A couple of strips of bacon that Elise
has been saving

Carrots that Celine chopped up for us

An onion from Mr. Ohland, or some cabbage

WHAT TO DO

Cook the bacon, add the onions.

Drain off the fat.

Throw in everything else.

*It's almost like stone soup.
The bigger the family, the more ingredients.*

XXXXXXXXXXXXXXXXXXXXXXXXXXXXXXXXXXXXXXXXXXXXXXXXXX

Chapter 25

Celine left in a flurry. Where was her sweater? Her hat? How would she manage to squeeze everything back into her suitcase?

Elise and I walked her to the subway, telling her to come back soon. I was surprised; I really would miss her.

"Don't forget your manners," Celine said at the subway entrance. "Be careful when you use the stove. . . ." She was still talking, still worrying as she disappeared down the steps.

I went down after her. "Call the stationery store, Celine, the minute you're home. I have to know you're safe."

I couldn't believe it. I was beginning to sound like her.

Elise and I grinned at each other; then we walked back to the bakery together. In the garden, the plums were ripe. I picked all I could reach so that Elise could bake a pie.

I spent most of the day with Mr. Ohland. We talked about the war and the peace that was surely coming. It was so warm that I sat at the edge of the pool, my feet dangling.

Late in the afternoon, the old man from the stationery store came to the door. I wasn't worried. I expected Celine's call. But still, when it came, I ran barefoot across the street to pick up the phone.

"Home," I said. "You're home."

"There's a telegram, Jayna. Two of them. Stuart said he didn't know where you were, or where I was."

I slid down against the wall, onto the floor.

"It's from the War Department," she said. "He gave it to me after all."

She was crying. I closed my eyes and braced myself. Would it take her forever to tell me about Rob?

But that wasn't what she said, not what the telegram said. He was alive. He'd been found on an island and had been recuperating in a hospital in the Philippines. He was coming home.

"And more, Jayna," Celine said. "The second telegram for you. From Rob himself."

I couldn't answer; I just nodded.

"'My dear sister, Jayna. I'm on my way home. We'll have soup!'"

Celine went on talking. "I telegrammed back immediately with the bakery's address so he knows where you are. He won't want to waste a minute getting to you."

After we'd hung up, I stayed against the wall, my head on my raised knees. All the waiting was almost over.

The old man came over and patted my shoulder. "Are you all right, Jayna?"

How surprised he was when I reached out and put my arms around his neck. Imagine! A man I hardly knew.

I danced across the street, into the bakery, and spun Elise around. "Alive!" I said. "Coming home!" I couldn't imagine words that were more beautiful.

⌇

The war ended on a hot sunny day in August. Kids banged pots and pans on Carey Street, church bells pealed, and fire engines clanged their horns.

Elise twirled me around the kitchen and pulled Mr. Ohland in with us. Ella was yapping excitedly and we were laughing, crying.

For days, I kept looking down the street, watching the entrance to the subway station.

But when Rob came, when he finally came, I didn't see him walking along Carey Street. I heard the bell in front, though, and Elise calling, "Jayna, I think he's here."

I reached for the curtain, pushed it open, and he ran toward me, yellow flowers in his hand.

After we hugged, hugged forever, I took the flowers. "You remembered that day at the pond." I looked up at him. "I knew you'd come."

He didn't answer. He just smiled. But I saw his eyes fill with tears.

We went outside to see Theresa in her new pool, and it didn't take long for everyone to be there with us. Andrew and Millie, Mr. Ohland and his pug, and Elise . . . of course, Elise.

I thought about the ghost and where she might be. Then I went back to the kitchen. I'd saved the recipe for this day.

XXX

Welcome-Home Soup

INGREDIENTS

A lot of fresh blueberries

Water

Sugar to taste

A bit of lemon (I like a lot.)

A couple of tablespoons of cornstarch

WHAT TO DO

Wash the blueberries. Get rid of any stems.

Eat a couple.

In a pot, cover the rest of the berries with water.

Add some sugar and the lemon.

Cook over low heat. DON'T BURN.

When the blueberries are soft, stir in the cornstarch.

Keep stirring until it thickens a bit.

You can serve it hot, cold, or medium!

XXXXXXXXXXXXXXXXXXXXXXXXXXXXXXXXXXXXXXXXXXXXXXXXXXXXX

MONTHS LATER . . .

᠌ↄ

I know what you're thinking. You believe there never was a ghost. After all, she had my ginger hair; she wore my nail polish and even my jacket with the silver buttons.

But listen to this. Just listen.

Rob and I went to Coney Island. We swam in the surf, our heads tilted up to catch the warm sun. Afterward, we sat on a blanket, eating the sandwiches and gingersnaps Elise had packed for us.

Would I tell him about the ghost? He always believed me.

But he had something to say first. "I was on that raft for weeks," he said. "Once in a while, I caught a fish. Sometimes it rained. But the sunburn was terrible, and the waves were high. And at last, I was ready to give up."

146

I shook my head, hardly able to swallow.

"But the oddest thing, Jayna," he said. "There in the middle of the ocean, I thought I saw a stone on the edge of the raft."

He looked at me. "Really, a stone."

"I believe you," I said.

"I reached out for it, but the raft was so unsteady, it rolled into the ocean. I remembered the funny little stone we'd found in the pond, and I knew I had to stay alive for you."

I was crying, crying again. How many tears had I shed in the last year?

Rob went on. "I sat up for the first time in days and saw green trees, an island, not so far. I managed to swim. I stayed alive until I was found."

I let the sun warm me. I knew we were going to stay in Brooklyn. I'd make soup for the bakery and we'd open a restaurant.

So there it is. Believe in the ghost or not. I send her my thoughts. I hope she hears them.

Oh, dear ghost, wherever you are resting at your silver lake, thank you. I do thank you.

Acknowledgments

Memories of my father, Bill, and my mother, Alice, first made me want to write this story. My father built lovely ponds in Lynbrook and Deposit, New York. My mother counted homecoming points for our neighbor's return from the war.

I owe an enormous debt to my cousin and lifelong friend, Ed Reilly, who generously shared his books about the war in the Pacific with me.

My son Jim said, "I knew you'd come," words that I cherish. My son Bill read the manuscript over and over, talking me through it. My daughter, Alice, was always there, supporting me and offering help.

As always, my editor, Wendy Lamb, was the source of tremendous encouragement and advice. Dana Carey, assistant editor, had many insights for me and lent me her name for the bakery on Carey Street.

Most of all, I must thank my dear husband, Jim, who served in the Pacific during World War II and told me his stories.

And I can't forget Brooklyn, home of my heart.

About the Author

PATRICIA REILLY GIFF is the author of many beloved books for children, including the Kids of the Polk Street School books, the Friends and Amigos books, and the Polka Dot Private Eye books. Several of her novels for older readers have been chosen as ALA-ALSC Notable Children's Books and ALA-YALSA Best Books for Young Adults. They include *The Gift of the Pirate Queen*; *All the Way Home*; *Water Street*; *Nory Ryan's Song*, a Society of Children's Book Writers and Illustrators Golden Kite Honor Book for Fiction; and the Newbery Honor Books *Lily's Crossing* and *Pictures of Hollis Woods*. *Lily's Crossing* was also chosen as a *Boston Globe–Horn Book* Honor Book. Her most recent books are *R My Name Is Rachel*, *Storyteller*, *Wild Girl*, and *Eleven*, as well as the Zigzag Kids series. She lives in Connecticut.

Patricia Reilly Giff is available for select readings and lectures. To inquire about a possible appearance, please contact the Random House Speakers Bureau at rhspeakers@randomhouse.com.